THE UNWINDING CORNER

THE UNWINDING CORNER

Alice Dwyer-Joyce

Chivers Press • Thorndike Press
Bath, England • Thorndike, Maine USA

KB VS IC DM WB MK VM FK CB VM

This Large Print edition is published by Chivers Press, England, and by Thorndike Press, USA.

Published in 1997 in the U.K. by arrangement with Robert Hale Ltd.

Published in 1997 in the U.S. by arrangement with Robert Hale Ltd.

U.K. Hardcover ISBN 0–7451–8968–7 (Chivers Large Print)
U.S. Softcover   ISBN 0–7862–1043–5 (General Series Edition)

The text of this Large Print edition is unabridged.
Other aspects of the book may vary from the original edition.

Set in 16 pt. New Times Roman.

Printed in Great Britain on acid-free paper.

British Library Cataloguing in Publication Data available

Library of Congress Cataloging-in-Publication Data

Dwyer-Joyce, Alice.
    The unwinding corner / Alice Dwyer-Joyce.
        p.   cm.
    ISBN 0–7862–1043–5 (lg. print : sc)
    1. Large type books.   I. Title.
[PR6054.W9U5   1997]
823'.914—dc21   96–53908

To my secretary, Mrs Bessie Jolley,
of Bar Hill, Cambridgeshire, for
working with great courage, in spite
of severe illness.

Before your glass last night you brushed
    your hair,
I saw you hesitate, look and with
    thoughtful fingers,
Trace the silver threads.
Wise wide eyes, looked back serene in
    years,
A sadness seemed to pass,
Too fleeting for the glass to catch.
And then was gone.
My darling, glance but in my soul and see
What you would wish.
For there the glass has caught and held,
You for ever.

                              Robert Dwyer-Joyce

PART ONE

THE CURLEW IN THE HILLS

Last night in my dreams, we had come to Merton House once again. We had driven up the country road, till we reached the top of the hill, where the Geraghtys lived, who opened our front gates. Bridie ran out of the half-door and frightened the fowls out of their wits. They had been scratching up the yard into a battlefield. They fled for their lives round the corner of the cottage and disappeared from our view. We could still hear their objections to our presence.

Bridie looked at me out of her long, green eyes, across the years, that were past and gone and I recalled how beautiful she had been as a growing child. If she had been washed and dressed in fine clothes, she could have been the prettiest of us all. As it was, her clothes were tattered and torn, too small or maybe too big for her. She looked at us with the hunger that is in a stray dog's eyes, and her feet were bare and dirty. She was glad to see me back, for it had been a long time. I could not think how long. She made the wrought-iron gates shrill out a welcome. We took the dog-cart through into the avenue and she closed the gates behind us.

'It's not the same at all, now ye're away,' she said in her old-fashioned way. 'The work isn't about these days and the happiness is gone out

3

of it, but they're at the hay again in the big front field. It's saved and ready to be taken into the barn, but I don't think it's real. It's too good to be real.'

At last we turned the corner round the damson tree and drove on through the outbuildings and there was a silence about the whole place. The big white house was very neglected. It had not been painted for years. The windows were not polished, not even opened. The path to the front door was carpeted with weeds. The front door wanted a coat of paint and the knocker had not been polished for ages and had run a line of verdigris from its brass.

I was well aware that the house inside was empty and echoing and that nobody came there any more. I knew that it was a dream from long ago. I had had it many times. I stayed with it. I had a love for it that I could never deny. If I touched the front door, it would have opened, but we drove up the back path, nearest the side door and came to Father's brass plate. I knew it so well, set in the wall of the dispensary, neglected, tarnished almost past reading.

John P Gregg, MD.

There was a flagged path along from the back door to the dispensary and the dispensary door was ajar and the place was not much changed

4

inside. I held onto the dream with grim fingers, as I stepped over the threshold. There was the kitchen table, the big white wood dresser, the boarded floor, with no pride of carpet. The boards had to be scrubbed every day. Father had gone. I could not remember, but in the dream, I always sought for him. I shut my eyes against the fading of a dream and against a waking-up. I clung to him still … willing myself to dreaming about all that had happened. I had always been welcome here, if he was not too busy. Always I could play in the dispensary, I always knew that. One day, I would become a physician, though ladies were not welcome in the professions.

Father said times would change and soon ladies would have the vote and ride bicycles and wear knicker-bockers, so why should they not enter the medical schools … even read the law and become 'silks'? I did not understand some of what he said, but he brightened up every time I came into that room and I shall never forget how it looked. There was no doubt that he kept me interested in the 'Art of Aesculapius' early on. I knew some of the secrets of the medical bag too. I might meet him on Marengo and going at a spanking trot in the high dog-cart, with the yellow wheels. I would be walking with Miss Hinchley, my governess. He might be going with the district nurse to help him and he would have the famous black bag. That damped my chances of going with him, because I was 'too young as yet'. Sometimes, he would sweep me up alongside himself and take me with him. He took me into a magic world. I might see a sick child, so that I could bring it cheer ... maybe I could see a baby that had arrived a week or so ago ... or an old lady, who just wanted a bright young face to make her smile again. Miss Hinchley did not approve of too much sick visiting on my part and said that I was spoilt, but Father and I were so taken up with each other, and I think the whole of Merton House approved. The best times were when he took me up in front of the saddle and we galloped for miles across the fields ... and came home more quietly, maybe at a lazy walk and talked about everything under the sun.

The whole countryside knew us. I might get a glass of raspberry vinegar from a big house or a mug of buttermilk or junket from the half-door of the cottage ... or perhaps a little basket of wild strawberries, picked at the rising of the day.

Always the rain held away and the sun shone and people were indulgent with us. The dispensary was the best thing of all. I wondered how long I could hide in the dream, for it was dear to me, this place. I remembered every bit of the dresser still. There were big coloured bottles on the shelves instead of plates, like the kitchen dresser had. These were special 'Winchester Quarts' for the stock mixtures, though they held far more than any quart. It was very handy the way Father compounded them concentrated strongly. He would put a little of the mixture in an eight ounce medicine bottle and fill the bottle up to the line at the top. It worked out to the correct dose of a tablespoonful, three times a day. You used clean water from the well to fill the Winchester. Then, when you made up the actual bottle of medicine, there was more pure water added.

'Shake well before taking'.

There was white paper for the wrapping and pink string for the tying and sealing wax for the pressing. The dispensary was a treasure house and it had a different smell from the rest of the house. There were liniments, and tinctures and shelves of ointment jars. The ointment had to be rubbed out on a marble slab. Powders must be pounded with a pestle in a bowl called a mortar. The cupboard held splints of different shapes for broken bones. I was proud that I knew that a 'cock-up splint' was for a broken wrist and that there was one for the right and one for the left forearm and that a break was called a fracture ... and a wrist fracture was a 'colles'.

One of my tasks was to tidy the dressings ... the cotton bandages, the tow, the cotton-wool, the lint. I had to keep the ointment boxes neat and make sure the labels had not got mixed up. The pill boxes were graded in size just so. There were labels for all classes of medicines and ointments and drops and chip ointment boxes.

To be well rubbed into the affected part
Not to be used in the eyes
The drops to be instilled into the
eyes/ears/nose ... morning and night.
Poison. Not to be taken internally.
And/Tablets ... One tablet to be taken three
times a day...
The dose not to be exceeded.

The Chippendale desk had been in the sitting-room, but Father had said it was not earning its keep. It took pride of place in the dispensary. Accounts were sent out on engraved note-paper.

Merton House
Ballyboy,
Longford.
Dr John Peacock Gregg
For professional services rendered...
Mrs Caroline Phillips, Screebogue House.
                                    Five guineas

Father always carried the essence of medicine with him. It was the mark of the doctor and the atmosphere of hospital and dispensary. Even now, if I visit a hospital or pharmacy or 'medical hall', I conjure up his memory. I spent hours in the dispensary but I never carried the same 'medical essence', Miss Hinchley saw to that. I was well scrubbed in a

8

hip bath in front of the nursery fire every evening with Pear's Toilet Soap.

She never objected to me playing in the dispensary any more than she minded if I played with the doll's house.

'The Master has but the one ewe lamb, when it's a parcel of sons he should have. It's a lonely part of the country and it's not often he sees another medical man all the year round. It does you no harm missie, but I doubt if you'll ever tread his footsteps, although that's what he wants for you. When you grow up, I daresay you'll find another medical man to wed. You can see to keeping his household for him and having his children and put all idea of being a doctor yourself out of your head. They don't want ladies interfering in medicine in Britain, nor yet in the law or having the vote. No lady would ever do the sort of nasty work a doctor has to do. They would not be real ladies, if they were to do that sort of thing. Oh, yes, I know there are some in America and there's talk of Garret Anderson and Sophia Jex-Blake. You'd be far better to stay up here in the nursery and do your lessons. Otherwise, go below to the kitchen and get the rudiments of running the house. Selina is a good cook and Marcella dotes on having you after her apron strings. She can show you how to wait at table and see to the linen and that. If you want to go out riding, Mick-Joe will only be too pleased to take you...'

I thought it all out; I would be a doctor like Father. I would have a carpet on the floor of the dispensary for a start ... not bare scrubbed boards. I lectured Miss Hinchley on the subject. If a person were ill, they want a bit of comfort under their feet ... There had been a day when she reiterated all her advice about my career and I had been arguing with her about the dispensary carpet. Memory was interfering with my dream.

'They come in muddy boots and bleeding all over the place. You can't have that on your fine carpet. They don't care where they throw off, Shanne. You could never have a carpet there ... maybe a bit of cork lino would satisfy Your Highness, but you'd get no thanks for it.' She looked at me severely. 'I'm only telling you the facts of life, Miss Shanne.'

There was no subject that held me like Medicine. I was like a chicken picking crumbs off the kitchen floor. I gathered this fact and that fact. I was greedy for knowledge, though perhaps it did me no good.

My dream was gone by this, or perhaps I had let it go. I imagined that Father was on his rounds, but I remembered the day that he was out and not expected back and Sheamus Geraghty had stepped on a broken jam-jar in the duck-pond at the back of their cottage yard. It was the first time I ever saw a severed main artery and I remembered it clearly. It

10

frightened me nigh death. Marcella always fainted at blood and she was stretched out on the kitchen floor in front of the big stove. Mrs Geraghty had brought Sheamus round to the back door, when she found the dispensary closed and her face was ashen. I was coming home from a walk and I went into the kitchen and came on the scene ... told Selina to burn feathers under Marcella's nose. It was the only thing I could think of when they said 'there was nobody on'. I trailed off into the dispensary and Mrs Geraghty with me and Sheamus.

I saw the picture of an arterial haemorrhage from the sole of a dirty foot. I wondered if Marcella were dead, or if the scorched feathers would restore her to her senses. Selina had the tail feathers of a fowl she had been preparing for the dinner. I turned my attention to the bleeding and its concise spurting jets ... not ordinary blood colour, but bright, bright, bright. Somehow I remembered the use of a tourniquet and how it was done. It was some sort of stricture, and it went either above or below the cut. Almost I had it. It went between the cut and then heart. Spurt ... spurt ... spurt, but bright, bright, red.

'You mustn't leave it on more than twenty minutes'. That was what Father had once said. I wished he would come back soon. I wasn't quite sure and it was my responsibility. 'Please make Father come home, before I go and let Sheamus die'.

11

'I think there's glass in it,' Mrs Geraghty muttered, and that was no help to me at all. 'He walked on a broken jam-jar and it nearly took the whole foot off of him. I think he's bleeding to death.' I had no doubt of it myself...

Selina deserted Marcella and came through to see what was happening, told us that Marcella was regaining her wits and not to worry.

'The Master'd have done that up tight,' she said. 'I can't recall how he does it, but he winds something about it and turns it like a windlass.'

I folded a triangular bandage into a strip and found a ruler on the desk. I did not know about a windlass, but anyway I twisted the ruler round to tighten the band and the bleeding stopped at once. All you had to do was to lay the ruler on the foot and twist a knot round about ... It was dead easy, I thought.

Selina was mopping up the spilt blood and I wondered what I should do after twenty minutes, if Father did not come home. My brain seemed quite empty of all the things I might have learnt. You let off the knot after the time was up, but if it bled again? Twenty minutes stretched out to eternity and I looked up at the clock. 'Tourniquet' that was the name of it.

'The time is up, Selina. It should have stopped now.'

Very gingerly, I loosened the constriction. The cut oozed a little and I felt a ton weight lift off my heart and I let out a great sigh. Yet the sound of my father's footsteps outside the door was maybe the most welcome sound I had heard in all my life.

He took in the whole situation at first glance.

'So it's Sheamus Geraghty in the wars as usual, Shanne? Wasn't it God himself who sent you in time? What have ye been doing to Marcella? There's a smell of burnt feathers in the kitchen and she's stretched out like a corpse in front of the stove . . .'

Sally Geraghty appeared at his side and said that Marcella was having a 'mag' and would be herself in time for the dinner. Father had taken Sheamus in his care and you could feel the relief in the household. Father was smiling at me and I knew his pride in me.

'I think it was an artery,' I said casually and he nodded his head, told me I had done well.

'You did my work for me, little Mouse. I've only to put a wee stitch in it now. You've done the important part. I thank 'ee.'

His eyes lit up with his love for me. That is how I will always remember him, and never cease my deep love for him. Nothing that happened down the years will ever change that.

Presently, the cut having been stitched and neatly bandaged, Father gave Mrs Geraghty and Sheamus a lift home to the gate-cottage in the dog-cart. He was careful to find Mother as soon as he came back and tell her that she had a fine daughter and she was to order a special cake for tea, with walnuts on it ... and white icing. It was a surprise, so she must not tell anybody but Selina. The memory of that cake was clinging to me, all mixed up with the old dream. There were filaments of what was always a variation of the same memory, misty and changing and given to cobwebs and gossamer. It came to be called my stock dream down all the years. I recognised it as part of my life ... perhaps a portent of my future.

Last night, the kitchen was the same enormous place with the wide fireplace that had the three-legged pot on the hearthstone. The pots hung on chains down the chimney. It was a long time ago. The fire had not been lit, nor the place scrubbed and tidied. The cupboards were empty and the whole place was thick with dust. The hall was neglected. It needed fresh wallpaper and shining paint. Only in dreams had I seen it so. The prim drawing room was formal as usual ... but the table was stacked with sets of china services, sheeted against the dust. The carpet was rolled up and the chairs piled, one on the other. The sitting-room was a far more informal place. The miniature conservatory fern in its small Crystal Palace had dropped the leaves and was quite dead. The clock on the mantle had stopped. The curtains had been taken down and the rooms seemed blind. The blinds were all gone and it was impossible. I tried to wonder if I was alone in the house. The rooms were deserted

14

and neglected. The furniture was stuck with auction numbers. There was an echo from the basement to the attics that made the hackles stand on the nape of my neck. Yet Bridie Geraghty had opened the gates of the avenue to us, just now. She had bounded along the side of the trap, as swift as a young kid goat ... and the slanted green eyes, not any different. I knew it was not true. Bridie was not a child any more. Father could not have been in the car with me and then appearing at the kitchen door in time to deal with an accident case. It was all out of order. Why was Merton House desolate, for that was the only word I could use. Sheamus Geraghty had cut his artery a long time ago. It was long past and Sheamus had joined the Irish Republican Army now and was a man of importance, who might carry a gun, against Britain and the Crown.

I tried to work out what time of the century it was, but I was lost. I had been born at the start of the nineteen hundreds ... nineteen hundred, the century itself. It was easy to remember, but folk said it was the same old trouble, said it had got worse instead of better. Yet I had been completely happy as the years went on. It had come, the new century, and all its hopes. I knew where I was at last, but as soon as I did, the dream picked up its skirts and ran away.

I had such a happy time from the day I was born. My happiness might run away like water through a sieve. It arrived with me, the new century. It did not seem possible that a brand new century might strike blow after blow.

I had been received into the Church at Tishinny. There had been a fashionable gathering for tea afterwards in the drawing-room at Merton House. I was in the nursery fast asleep, of course but, at last, I was brought down and presented to the company in that lovely room I knew so well afterwards. There was such a company that we had to spread into the sitting-room, where the fern grew in the Crystal Palace. It stood in the low window and filtered the light. In a year or two, Mother must have started making the raspberry vinegar. It was kept in the cupboard there. On my birthday, the raspberry vinegar had not been thought of ... nor the raspberry canes planted in the garden. Enough years had not gone by yet. James Byrnes, our landlord, was a great expert on raspberries. It is quite possible that he peeped out into the garden and thought it would be a good place to grow them and in the course of time, so they were to be grown. The cupboard in the wall would store raspberry vinegar perfectly. All that had to be done was the making of it each year and the picking of the raspberries was my responsibility. Mick-Joe, Father's man, would have set the canes. He had a whole household to encourage him. In the kitchen, Selina, the cook, in a white apron and a mob-cap, was the expert and an authority. Marcella was the house-

16

parlourmaid and a tall, handsome girl with two black ribbon streamers down her back and her hair braided neatly. She had a sharp, smart way with her. Sally Geraghty was a scrawny hungry girl, eldest daughter of the gate-cottage ... and our kitchen-maid. She slept in, for there was no room for her at home. Selina said that Sally was a great one for finishing up the broken meats. She was always one for scraping mixing bowls and cake mixtures, but she was a good worker ... always willing for any job that had to be done and as good as two men out in the yard, so Selina said. Sally herself had told me that she had a new dress for the christening, in crisp cotton, striped like a sugar stick. Of course, Sally was the sister of Sheamus and Bridie. The mother was a widow. The father had given his life for Britain in one of the South African wars.

A 'monthly' nurse came to live in, when I was due to be born. She went away after a month, for her time was up and it was a great relief when Miss Hinchley came. She was to be my governess and I liked her very much, or they said I did. She knew what went on. It was she who gave me the best account of the christening. There had been great excitement at the accident, or so she told me. She had not been there, but she had 'heard tell'.

There had been an accident on the Ballymahon road with an outside car of drunken farmers overturned into a ditch, going home from the fair. My father had to go. Mick-Joe was waiting with the trap. Two more doctors from the company went to help him, mighty glad to escape the polite company. By the time they had cleared up the whole affair and got home safely again, my birthday celebration had come to a close. I was just a new baby and my glory had departed, because I had started to cry and had been removed from the company.

It was all over, yet that was only the beginning.

I have the story of my infant years, so perhaps we can be done with dreams. Merton House was a gentle kingdom with Father as King, and Mother, Queen. It was a paradise to me and life was gentle and slow. The family always regarded Mother as a beauty and Father adored her. First of all, I knew her as the pretty lady who came to read me stories at bedtime. The scent of honeysuckle always brings her back and I can imagine Sally in the sitting-room, helping her with the Crystal Palace fern under the bow window. Sally Geraghty had green fingers, not that I ever thought she had. Usually they were black from the polish of the knives or the blacking of the grates—the eternal scrubbing of floors. Her hands looked like fresh shrimps netted from the sea in Galway Bay.

I had been born at the turn of the century and things had started to move in Ireland. But I

18

did not know it.

The veteran loco No 36 was busy hauling trains on the Great Southern and Western Railways, between Dublin and Cork. The country was opening up to the Industrial Revolution. Then there were the Transvaal and the Orange Free State and the wars, but the wars were across the ocean a long way. Merton House dreamed in the bog lands of Longford. It was a hungry enough land. Mostly near Merton was turbary. There the heather and the unreclaimed shivering peat stretched for miles. At the back of the house, there was a spring of fresh water and plumbing was unknown. The water was fetched in galvanised buckets and stood on the scrubbed kitchen table, crystal pure, with a zinc dipper handy in case you wanted a drink. Nobody seemed to think it strange that frogs inhabited the well and the little stream that flowed down from it and wandered, dressed with cresses and away through the beauty of the turbary. Nobody thought it strange to use the little house, two hundred yards along a path from the kitchen door. In there, was a seat with two holes, a bucket of ashes to shovel down, a nail in the wall, newspapers, cut in squares and perforated, threaded with string. It was a way of life in the early part of the century. We were planning for a new world. There was no future for wars. In 1905, I looked to the front and knew no fear. I was Shanne Gregg and I had everything life could spread out before me. The quiet river was rich with water-lilies and there were trout in its cool depths. The hay field was cut and stacked and ready for the barn. The valley stood so thick with corn, that it did laugh and sing ... or would do so presently. It must go on for ever.

Then I had a pony called Tea-Leaf and rode on a leading-rein to start. Mick-Joe saw to it all ... a Barry Fitzgerald of a man. He would stand no nonsense. No, I could not start riding to hounds yet, though I was past six and thought I was my own mistress now. In no time at all, I was off the leading-rein, but that did not mean anything. 'Miss Shanne, if you bring the little mare in, in a sweat, 'tis yourself will be walking the yards with her, till she cools off. If she comes in petrified with cold in the harsh days, you'll give her warm bran mash and rub her down, till her ears is warm. See to her comfort, before you even think of your own and don't let me catch you doing any different.'

Behind the house was the fairy land of Merton, where they cut and dried the turf. From there, it was carted into the turf-shed, or stacked in a clump near the back door. It filled Merton with the smell of Ireland and smoked through the chimneys, so that I will never forget any more than any Irish woman will, this incense carried to the skies.

The front avenue wound through big fields and down near the house were trees ... a forest of oaks and ash and elms. At the back came the outbuildings, stables and to spare and barns and hen-houses and the harness rooms and the turf-sheds, and the carriage houses. I remembered it as a busy place, not as it always was in the dream desolate.

There was a walled garden, well-stocked. I always recall the damson tree, for it was for climbing. Selina made damson jam every year and restocked the jam cupboard.

There were raspberry canes in the garden too and that meant raspberry jam and better still raspberry vinegar to drink. Miss Hinchley and I were the fruit pickers and looking back I can recall gooseberries and black and red currants and crab apple jelly ... all the jellies, that had to be strained through a funnel of real flannel. I had a very busy time. I cannot remember idleness. Perhaps it was not tolerated. I had duties in the dispensary and I took them very seriously, maybe got hooked on medicine that way, but as the years passed Father elected me as a sick visitor for the practice too. It all made for adventure. It meant that I could take Tea-Leaf and visit one of the patients who was ill and in Father's care. It was usual to bring a little gift, tobacco for the men and maybe tea for the ladies. Mostly I went to the elderly, who were house-bound, and they looked forward to my visits. I came to realise that perhaps they sat in the same chair in the corner, all the day every day, till I came back again, but they were

21

usually the centre of a big family. I worked at it quite a bit. A bunch of lily-of-the-valley was a treasure to an old lady, who sat in a thatched cabin, that had no luxuries, but it was the fact that she could tell me all about her three sons, who had gone to South Africa and never come back. It was better so. They had joined the South African Police after the war and they were making fortunes. They had sent her an ostrich egg and one day they would come and see her. There was nothing for them in Ireland any more. You couldn't earn a living.

My father took a gold sovereign from his pocket one day in the dispensary and spun it across the room to me and I caught it like a kitten.

'That's what they want,' he said. 'I'm not saying that the flowers and the damson jams and the quarters of tea don't show willing, but what the nation wants is a good working wage and food in their stomachs as a right. Their stomachs are lean. Not charity, for God's sake! There are so many children to feed ... so many mouths and not enough food for them, not on agricultural wages in this day and age. Ireland wants self-government and even now, they're working for it, like moles under the ground. The curlews are in the hills as yet, but God knows how much strife we'll have before the Irish peasant children don't run barefoot.'

I came to learn the history of the famine, but it meant little to me. I was always dressed in fine warm clothes and had a new riding-habit down from Callaghan's in Dame Street in Dublin. It was important to learn to sit a horse. I was off the leading-rein and I was free to go with anybody who would take me . . . Mick-Joe or Father or Mother. I could go to do the messages by myself along the cross-roads in Carrickboy. I was allowed to dine in the dining-room now with Mother and Father and Miss Hinchley. I was growing up. I went out in the governess car to visit with Mother, to visit our friends in the big ascendancy houses round about. It was like Cranford, run just as primly. There were the Byrnes family, our landlords on the hill . . . Miss Byrnes and her brother 'Mr James,' who owned all the land around. Mother and I would drive up by road and take tea and it was all very boring to me. Mr James might step in to take a dish of tea and talk to me about my lessons.

'It's time for your tincture,' Miss Byrnes would say and give him a dram of Irish whiskey. Mother and I might indulge in some of the elderberry wine. Perhaps we would take just a sip of this new year's vintage? Maybe it was a way of life that was soon to end . . . damson wine and seed cake. To me, it seemed as if it would go on for ever, but I have found nothing ever does, even Miss Byrnes's interminable 'Afternoon at Home Days'.

I did not know that 1914 was the beginning of the end of all the quiet life. I had scampered freely around the environs of Merton House and had grown to teenage. I was as old as the century. It was easy to remember and life moved in happiness with the roses blooming and the bees buzzing in the heather and the honey slow in the comb and the gorse a glory on the peat bogs.

Life changed for me, as it would do for so many people. Maybe there were warnings that I did not notice ... the feeling of a storm coming up. Surely the Great War was storm enough to blow away half the world?

It started when Austria declared war on Serbia, July 28th, 1914. The heir to the Austrian throne had been assassinated at Sarajevo. It meant nothing to me except a boredom of political talk between the men over the dinner tables. As I said, Miss Hinchley and I had the honour of dining officially now and it *was* counted high honour. Selina was kind enough to say I 'had the right use of my knife and fork and I could appear without making a holy show of myself, was I not Miss Shanne Gregg—the doctor's only daughter, but when they talked war, it would be better if I held my tongue, for I don't know what I was talking about'.

It was getting closer. Britain declared war on Germany on 4th August, but it would be over by Christmas and I was not to bother my head. I worried that the military might come and take Tea-Leaf away ... give her to the cavalry, burn a brand on her rump ... the broad arrow of a convict. Tea-Leaf was my polo-size pony. Still, maybe Russia and France were at war. On 23rd August, 1914, the first battle of Mons opened its guns, but nobody from the War Office had been to buy up our horses and Tea-Leaf was safe from having to charge through the smoke of battle. She was safe for now. The first Meet of the season was coming. Father still reckoned to hunt at least two days a week. It was the usual habit of the medical practitioners and the parsons. Mick-Joe saw to it that it was routine in the stable-yard. Mother never knew fear out hunting. Mick-Joe was her whipper-in. It was a great joke. I recall how she laughed at it. She knew she must not gallop over the hounds. When did she ever do such a thing? She had full control of Lady Gay. Just let Michael-Joe tell her one time, when she ever lost control of her mount.

I remember the silver laugh and Mick-Joe sullen with us all. It would be my first day out with the full hunt soon and the talk of Mons just a cloud in the sky. Surely Mons was not going to be allowed to interfere with the hunting?

There were casualties coming in from France. Miss Byrnes had started a thing called 'The Red Cross'. We were expected to go to her house every Thursday for tea and to roll cotton bandages. We must learn first aid and home nursing. All the teen-aged girls from the big houses had to volunteer. There was no option. I was enrolled without delay and wore a nurse's uniform in Tishinny Church on Sunday evening's church and we all sat in the front row, very proud. I was taking my place in the war effort, but I was more interested in my first day at hounds. The Meet was to be at Merton House. Mick-Joe put me up in my saddle and me with no care in the world for the war. I glanced round at the assembled company in the front avenue. The dream was fading at last, but I did not know it.

Yet still down the years I dream it and recognise it and know that I can wrap it round me like a cloak ... the old happiness. I can cast it aside too, as if I exorcise an evil spirit from my brain.

The autumn sun was shining on the hunting pink of the gentlemen. The ladies looked elegant, with their immaculate white stocks and burnished boots. Mother was sitting side-saddle, her top hat veiled securely to her head, flattering to her face. She kept me close to her and our lives ran brightly and happily together. My heart thumped with excitement and Tea-Leaf was dancing with mischief...

Marcella and Sally Geraghty were circulating the company with stirrup cups on silver trays ... cherry brandy, whiskey, sherry wine. Sally slipped a little silver chalice of cherry brandy to me and I saw the wistful envy in her eyes. The syrup was very strong and foreign to my palate, but I knew I had maybe come of age. It was a milestone crossed and Mick-Joe told me it was good for 'the courage'.

'Not that you'll need it, Miss Shanne. Sure, you're a real lioness, so you are.'

I shall hate the taste of cherry brandy till the day I die. Always it recalls the nightmare horror sequence, just as bright and sharp, as it was then. I smiled at Mother across the brim of the cup and she wrinkled her nose in mock disapproval, but she did not disapprove at all.

'Courage, ma petite!' she said and it was all bright laughter, though the gentlemen were trying to group together and talk politics still. The hounds were keen to go. The horses were too impatient to stand talking about war. They jostled together for position and were sweating to be away ... jinking their bits and snatching at the steel. Then the hounds were off on a breast-high scent and Tea-Leaf was not going to wait. Mick-Joe was screeching at Mother to keep clear of the wood, but Lady Gay had taken the bit between her teeth and had plunged straight ahead. A cock pheasant got up from the brush and straight into her face and Lady Gay was away.

'Make for the hill, Ma'am.'

She was off along the forest ride, with me on her heels. I had no choice. Tea-Leaf was not going to leave her stable companion even if I sawed the bit across her mouth. It happened so quickly to change our whole way of life. All I

27

knew was that the grey had bolted and that there was no holding the pony. Mick-Joe had headed her off and he had her by the rein now. He had turned us aside. Perhaps fate had made the big oak tree grow just so. Its branches scooped Mother up. Father wheeled back to help but it was too late. Mother cannot even have seen the branch that struck her temple. She was thrown down like a rag-doll, thrown by a careless child.

The silk top-hat was off her head, the veil torn and blood on her face ... her arm was outflung and very still, neck turned away as if she did not want to see what had happened ... still, still, still. I do not know how I came to be kneeling by her, but I was trying to get my gloves off, trying to find my handkerchief. I saw the bloodstain and knew that she did not move ... did not talk to me. Her eyes were shut, as if she slept. Then Father was kneeling down beside her and I got a great sense of relief. I knew he would make her well. There was no expression on his face as he bent forward and lifted an eye-lid. I was there and very frightened, but he did not notice me. His face was of stone, as he told some of the men to take a gate off its hinges. There seemed no movement any more. Even the bleeding had stopped, but the blood was still red on the handkerchief. The bleeding had stopped, but Mick-Joe was bending down over her, his face like a dead man's.

His cap was in his hand and he made the sign of the cross on his breast.

'She's done for, the Mistress. May her soul rest in peace.'

I thought how grey his hair was in the autumn sun and the tears in his voice as he bent his lips to Mother's ear.

'Oh, my God, I am heartily sorry for having offended Thee. I detest my sins above every other evil, because they displease Thee, Oh, my God!'

It was the Act of Contrition. I knew it was all over, or maybe just beginning. Men had lifted Mother onto the field gate and were carrying her slowly home. Father walked beside them and I went to run after him, but Mick-Joe's hand held me back, his arm tightly about me. 'Let Himself alone now. There goes his life and all he ever lived for.'

He drew a deep sigh from his broad chest.

'I have your mare waiting. Let me put you up into the saddle and let you ride home to the woman-kind. They'll know they the way to comfort you. Himself will want a brave daughter, to see him through the days to come. Don't make it harder for him by putting your loss before his. Even if you've lost your mother, his is the greatest disaster. You're only a child now and the tears are hot in your throat and running down your face, but isn't your whole life in front of you for the living? Look at the Master, walking behind the rest of his life.

Go home now and don't dry your tears too quick. Weep awhile for Herself and then start preparing to be the mistress of Merton House.' He looked at me, his face drenched in sorrow. 'Mistress of Merton, Miss Shanne, and may God inspire you!'

I watched Father walk slowly back behind the field gate, knowing that nothing would ever be the same again. Perhaps it was the same in the whole world in 1914, at the first Battle of Mons, everything changed.

The house was dark presently with all the blinds drawn down. I thought it could not be really happening. They had dressed Mamma in a white lace night-gown and she lay, as if she slept, in the master bedroom, in the big old four-poster bed. There was a heavy fragrance of flowers in the room and people who came to pray and weep. Yet the house was dark indeed and such silence of whispers and business of callers. Gradually the tiled floor of the hall was carpeted with wreaths. People came to walk up the stair and say 'the funeral oration'.

'She was a gracious lady, God rest her! Her fist was never closed to the poor.'

That was poor Mrs Geraghty, who lived in our gate lodge cottage and her daughter, Sally, had taken her up the stairs and Sally grabbed my hand in hers for comfort and made it hard for me not to cry. I got the way of it eventually. The Catholics knelt down and prayed for Mother's soul. The Protestants were not permitted that comfort, but I knew that already and was sorry for it. The Protestants all wore their Sunday clothes and kissed me and said I must ask if there was anything they could do to help in any way. It was a good thing I had nearly grown up, but I was still very young to take the responsibilities that must be mine now. Of course, Miss Hinchley would guide me as she had always done ... etc, etc, etc.

So I was fourteen turned and the world war was well on its way. My hair was in two plaits down my shoulders, tied with black ribbons. I had a new black dress, made by the dress-maker, who called for the purpose and she made it full length, with instructions and all their faces turned to me, when I appeared in the long dress—Selina's, Marcella's, Sally's, Mick-Joe's, even Miss Hinchley's. There was no question that any of them challenged my authority. Father picked up the keys from the kitchen dresser and put them in my hand. Then he went off to the dispensary but when I followed him, I heard the key click on the lock. Thereafter I groped for answers and found few ... kept my own counsel.

The day of the funeral, the undertaker called me Miss Gregg and I wondered who he meant. I was in the black broadcloth dress and the sempstress was laying a black seal stole around my shoulders. Miss Byrnes had come upstairs to see I was ready. I was sitting in front of the mirror and she looked at me without a word.

31

She picked the stole off my neck and flung it on the dressing table. Then she twisted the braids of hair behind my head into a chignon. She went out of the room and was back again in half a minute. I recognised one of Mother's hunting hats and one of her graceful veils. I stretched out my hands to protest, but then I saw my reflection in the mirror. Surely it was Mother who looked back at me? I was grown up in a split second of time and Miss Byrnes's voice whispering in my ear.

'She'd have liked it best of anything. She was my oldest friend. Who would want to see you in that matronly stole, when you could grow up to look like this. She has been my best friend. Take a grip on yourself, Shanne Gregg, for half the county is out there. They have some of the hounds too, to do her honour...'

Why did people not warn me? I was armoured against weeping. Through the landing window, I saw the four black horses tossing their plumes and pawing the gravel of the drive, impatient to be gone. I saw the long line of wreaths down the hall and out along the path and beyond them, the line of the carriages in the drive. It was the moment when I grew up, but it was the old story of the Art of Medicine. Selina stood in the hall.

'We're in terrible trouble with Mrs Geraghty's Bridie. She's dropped the flat-iron on her finger and it's ruined on her.'

I found myself in the dispensary and indeed

32

Bridie was there with her mother. I drew comfort that the old dispensary was unchanged. It was the same place and my father already dealing with Bridie. Mrs Geraghty's face was ashen at the sight of me in my grown-up disguise and she poured out an apology to Father, that he did not even comprehend, as I came in.

Mist. gent cum.rhei. Mist pertussis pro infant. Mist ferri.et ammon.cit ... the same familiar surety of help. Yet my mind was in turmoil. A sharp blow from an old tree on the temple. In the twinkling of an eye it could happen and medicine was put to nought. Father's face was drawn, when he looked at me and saw Mother again in me. I was terrified suddenly, as I went to him for help.

'She could never be happy in heaven without us, Father. Surely she will explain to God and he'll let her come back.'

He put me away from him and indeed Mrs Geraghty drew back from me. A hound outside set up a mournful howl and Bridie crossed herself. Mrs Geraghty told me that if I didn't take care, I'd put the evil eye on my own mother and she crossed herself too.

'Do you want your sainted mother to be walking Merton House for eternity? Let her lay at peace with the blessed dead.'

Bridie had dropped the heavy iron on her finger. It was a blood blister and it should be punctured with a hot needle. Father had the needle held in the flame and the glow of it was terrifying Bridie out of her senses.

'It doesn't hurt,' I told her ... 'not a bit. It just stops all the pain and that's an end of it.'

I remember the slow tears and the smell of burning horn.

'I'm sorry, Miss Shanne, I wouldn't have put more trouble on you.' There was a spurt of blood and the pain was gone, but it was time for the coffin to be carried down. I watched it being slid into the hearse and the wreaths arranged and the sweetness of them. Father had gone into the dining-room and was drinking a full glass of very amber whiskey. Then he had come to stand by me and again he seemed to flinch at the side of a grown-up daughter, that maybe he had thought was dead ... and somebody who was dead and gone for ever. In a small moment of time, I found Bridie at my side and tears on her face and no handkerchief to wipe them away. I gave her mine and was sorry for her sorrow.

'I know the pain that's come to ye,' she whispered. 'Don't want the Mistress back. My Dad was killed in Africa in the war and we wanted him back, but he never come. There's no way to get a soul back, no matter how you pray for it. Wars is bad.'

It was time for Father and I to get into the first coach. I put my arm in his and together we went.

'You're very like her, Shanne...' he said and

34

no more.

The long cortege was moving off, but first went the walking people, before the coffin, mostly the poor from all the country around. I heard for the first time 'the Irish cry', the wailing of the women of Ireland for their dead. There were so many of them ... in best Sunday Mass clothes and in shawls. It was a cry that pierced the heart with sorrow. After the walkers came the rich carriages, one after the other ... and the chiming of the hounds, muted and kept under tight control ... the few men in pink coats, a sharp crack of the lash now and again and a cry of command...

There seemed to be no reality to Mother's funeral. I could not realise it was actually happening. The grey mare was led behind the hearse by Mick-Joe with the side-saddle and the bridle polished and shining, the reins that awaited her hand never again.

I collected snatches of the service ... the carrying of the coffin up the centre aisle to lie on trestles before the altar in the chancel ... the cross of white roses on her breast.

'I am the resurrection and the life' saith the Lord. 'He that believeth in me, though he were dead, yet shall he live and he that liveth and believeth in me, shall never die.'

'I know that my Redeemer liveth...'

I had a little posy of honeysuckle in my hand and I had been told that I must follow the hearse to the graveside and presently I must throw down the flowers to the top of the coffin. There was a brass plate ... *LOUISE GREGG 1878–1914.*

It was a steep little path up to the open grave and the undertaker was used to ceremony. The dug grave had been lined with tendrils of ivy and there were bands for lowering the coffin gently into its place. Father leaned heavily on my arm and Miss Hinchley whispered in my ear.

'You're the strong one. You must be brave.'

Looking down the hill, I could see all the carriages with the ladies waiting for it all to be over. The grooms were having a job to keep the horses in order. They fretted at their bits and pawed up the gravel of the Church avenue. The humbler people had tied their traps to the wooden fence. There were one or two donkey carts. Ah yes! She had loved donkeys and had been their champion and this I knew. It was right that the donkeys had come. The women had started to keen again and it was agony to me ... a moaning of pain against the skies of all the sorrows they had known in their poor lives. It was a cry of anguish at what the women of Ireland had had to bear. Maybe I did not know it then, but I came to understand it before I was finished. Ireland was a most distressful country ... 'the most distressful country that I had ever seen, for they're hanging men and women for the wearing of the green'. I was to see it. I was to know it. Just for now, I threw down the honeysuckle, a dart of fragrance through the clear bright air, to lie on the brass of her name.

'Ashes to ashes and dust to dust.'

There was a fall of dust to the coffin and I could go now. Mick-Joe, leading Mother's mare, was waiting for me at the bottom of the hill and he fended off people who sought to detain me. He held the iron for me and set me in the saddle, whispered to me that the rector had charge of Father and I was free to go with himself ... turned off through a spinney of trees.

'I should have gone back with Father.'

'The Protestant clergyman will look after him. You don't want to get mixed up with all those fine folk. Canon Webster will be filling out the hard stuff in Waterford goblets. Over in Merton House, the women will have trays of sandwiches and biscuits and cakes ... enough to feed the poor of the parish. The men will still talk about war. They say the wounded men is flowing in from Mons like a river from the mountains. Did you know that Carrickboy House has offered the place as a convalescent home for wounded officers straight from the lines?' He turned Lady Gay off through a small coppice of rowan trees and down a little hill.

'Nobody will miss you, Miss Shanne. This war in France is bigger than the funeral of a fine lady ... and that she was. Carrickboy is to be a convalescent home for officers. The trench fighting is new. We don't understand it, but it's

37

a new sort of making war … and this is brutal war, your mother's death was swift and happy.'

After a silence he went on.

'This war ain't going to be over for a long time, not this side of Christmas like they all say. It's time you and I had a talk for there's a cloud coming up the skies of Ireland, such as we've maybe never seen in all our lives. We'll take the long way home to Merton, Miss. 'Tis time for yourself and myself to be talking. You're better out of the crush they'll have in the drawing-room at home.'

They were lanes he knew and the nuts past ripening and fallen from the hazel bushes and the blackberries were past the picking this year. The land that was used for peat was incredibly beautiful, even if the rowans had shed their berries. The holes where the turf had been taken had filled with indigo water. The turf itself was stacked in dark brown steps, angled one against another, to dry out. Soon, the blocks of peat would be collected and brought home, to the white cottages.

'If you were to come this way another time, you'd want to mind where Tea-Leaf would be threading her way, Miss Shanne. Some of these holes do go down to the centre of the earth. It's easy to be drowned here and the weed green in your hair.'

He was very sad. He wanted to speak to me so badly that he had kidnapped me from

38

Mother's funeral. He knew the country like the palm of his hand and he had worked his way round to a small copse, that had rabbits running on it on a little furzy hill, bright with the gorse. He folded his coat for me to sit on and took out his pipe and asked my permission to smoke, took long enough to fill the pipe with plug.

'I daresay you haven't been interested in the war?' he said. 'But 'tis on us now and there'll be trouble for every man Jack of us. There's going to be no living the way we done ... not now. Our own world in Merton House's been turned upside down. It will never be the same any more. We're not alone. The whole world's been turned upside down. Life will never be the same again as I said, no matter how long we live ...'

Mick-Joe had fought in the last South African wars. He was an ex-British soldier, growing iron-grey now and old in my eyes.

'Maybe it's time you grew up,' he remarked. 'You will have to take your right place in Merton, as the Mistress and do the best you can. It's a pity that the Mistress was taken before there was time for you to have wed and have a place of your own. It was a pity that the Mistress wasn't spared to see her gran' childer under her feet. That's the order of things, but they fell out awry. It ain't natural. You should have been wed and had your own house ... before the devil sent this misfortune. God have mercy on us!'

39

He sat down on the fallen trunk of a tree and pulled hard on the shag in the pipe, till it glowed warmly.

'Maybe, 'tis time you grew up,' he said again. 'Maybe 'tis Ireland I'm fretting about and not how you'll manage the house. You'll be able for that. You'll take your place as Mistress for now, but maybe you don't know that we're a distressful country in Ireland. For a long time, there's been a boiling-up of trouble agen the Crown and a seeking for home-rule ... and men jealous to be their own masters.'

'I'm not interested in politics,' I said, and he told me I had better be.

'Far be it from me to put more trouble on your shoulders, Miss Shanne. You have trouble in plenty now, but there are men in the hills against Britain, with guns pointed against Britain. They're drilling to carry arms. God send they don't move soon, but they're getting ready to go ... not yet, please God, but it will come.

'Give it a year or two and a strange new army will rise up against the British Army ... and these same soldiers are their own brothers ... ones like me, that went out against Africa and won agen the Boers.'

I had no worry against a rebellion in Longford. We were a long way from the Somme and all the fighting. Miss Byrnes had introduced home nursing and first aid classes twice a week in her house on the hill and she had enlisted many of us 'young ladies', but Mother's death had snuffed all my interest in it. I had heard talk of a convalescent home for officers, that was to be established in Screebogue House, Lieutenant Colonel Toby Phillips' big house. I was surprised that Mick-Joe could bother me with more worry, but he went on with it and his pipe went out on him and I thought it served him right.

'There's a whisper of a rising to come, Miss Shanne ... give it two years or so and the Irish Republican Army will rise against the British Crown. They're only a handful of young men now, but they're lit with the flame of Irish Independence. It has happened all down the years and always they've failed, but they're gathering like curlews in the hills ... training in the lonely wild places ... just waiting. They will rise to attack the British Army and force terms on Britain. It is time you understood the tar smearings that appear on the gentry's gates ...'

I worried about running the house. How could I listen to such talk? I was friendly with all my neighbours and with 'the Poor of the Parish'. I knew they liked me. Longford was a long way from the war. I gathered up all my efforts to try to run the house as Mother had done. Mother had made it look easy and it was easy, with all the help she had had, and I still had.

'I hope the Master won't run off to join the British expeditionary force,' Mick-Joe muttered gloomily. 'He'd take me and maybe two of the horses and then the fat would be in the fire.'

He drew a deep sigh.

'What he wants is a good widow-woman for a housekeeper. Let you go on with your growing-up to be a lady.'

'I'll see to the house. He'll be happy again, but the house will miss Mother. If we have a rebellion as well, Mick-Joe, God only knows what will become of us all, but it's all kitchen talk, so tell me what Irish Independence is.'

''Tis government of Ireland by the Irish people themselves. 'Tis freedom!' he said. 'You can't be that ignorant Miss Shanne?'

I knew vaguely that Ireland had been fighting for her freedom for three hundred years—sometimes they said seven hundred years. I didn't know for sure. The Catholic schools taught it, but not the sort of schools Protestants attended and certainly not the genteel places where I picked up my education … after-hour lessons with the Model school teacher and with Miss Hinchley, and with the rector…

'You know that's rebel stuff, Mick-Joe … the Fenians and the Battle of the Boyne and the Siege of Limerick and all the nonsense about Cromwell. Besides, Mother is dead and we have no right to be talking politics today. Yet, I'd like to believe about General Sarsfield and the grand hero they make him … how he

42

surrendered and then the French sent help. "The French are in the Bay," they said, but he had surrendered and it was too late. He could have won, but he would not withdraw his word and the British honoured him for it. The legend says that they let him march out of Limerick with full military honours and the colours flying and the fifes playing ... and to the beat of the drum. They become the best mercenary soldiers that were ever to be ... and were called the "Wild Geese".'

'And where did ye hear the like of that?' he asked me and I told him I had it from Bridie Geraghty one day in the kitchen.

Actually she had given me her word it was true and she had been very dramatic about it. She had been cleaning the knives on the board with bathbrick ... and she had nicked her finger and the blood was as red-pink as a white mouse's eye.

She looked at me and told me that General Sarsfield had been killed years later by some sort of a horrible sabre cut. He had been very sad as he died on the field at Landen and he had looked at the blood and said 'Oh, that this blood been shed for Ireland'.

'Is that so?' Mick-Joe said. 'You have a red-hot rebel in that little green-eyed she-goat.'

'She said they told her about it in the convent,' I said defensively and he told me dryly that the holy sisters said more than their prayers and our arguments dwindled and died.

After a while he tapped out his cold pipe and put it away with a sigh.

'We'll talk no more about it, Honey,' he said. 'Just hold it in your head, that I'm your man. Keep a still tongue above all. The rebels have been sleeping, but they'll wake soon. Know it for a fact that they're arming and maybe it's a pity that the Crown is at war already. Maybe we're going to stab an old enemy in the back, for we're fighting for Britain here, some of us. You're caught up in it too and it's cruel. You're Protestant-British, yet you're Irish born and Ireland is your country, but there are people who think a Protestant can't be Irish and that's Tommy rot. Robert Emmet was a Protestant and Wolfe Tone too, and they gave their lives for Britain. You're Miss-Facing-Both-Ways. You'll be torn apart by the storm that's coming. God have pity on you! You'll be like the infant child that was brought to judgment before Solomon. I want to say to you in all secrecy, keep this in your head, when you see the flames go up the skies and hear the rifles in the streets and the fine houses burning round your ears.'

He made a step with his two hands to put me in the saddle and then he led me away across the peat lands.

'It's time we turned for home, Acushla.'

He squinted up at me against the setting sun, his shrewd eyes like the agates in Mother's ring.

'They'll all be gone home, if we don't make

44

haste. You have to bid them goodbye and thank them. Then we will draw up the blinds and start again ... let the light in ... just one word more. My loyalty is for Merton House and its people. It's not that I'm a red-hot Republican like Bridie Geraghty and her like. I fought for a soldier in South Africa, as your father's batman. There's many of us, Facing-Both-Ways, like you are yourself. You're British-Ascendancy and you have dual nationality here. It's the way it was. Miss Byrnes has you at the Red Cross and the home nursing and that stamps you for Protestants and Britain, yet I know your heart is for Ireland. If Ireland were to start rebellion agen the Crown for freedom, it would be a queer state of affairs for both yourself and myself.'

There is no need to recapitulate the dregs of the funeral and the gradual emptying out of the drawing-room and the sitting-room ... the trays of drinks, as if it were a Meet of hounds ... the silver trays of small cakes and cups of tea. It went on for an awfully long time. The solicitor wanted to speak to me. He took me away to Father's study. Father was lying down in the library, deep in an armchair and people were too kind to say he was drunk.

The solicitor talked to me patiently and I did not understand one half of what he said. He went as far as to ask my permission to have Mick-Joe present and I was glad of it, yet still I did not understand.

45

The guests had all driven off in their carriages. The maids had cleared up the rooms and were sitting round the open range in the kitchen with a big brown pot of tea warming on the hob. I listened carefully to Mr Mitchell and could not collect my wits. It seemed that Father's affairs were in a poor state. He had always been careless in keeping his books. He believed in running accounts with the rich to pay the poor. The rich were 'bad pays'. His banking was overdrawn. Mr Mitchell had a cure for the condition, for Father believed in keeping on all the servants. 'If I had the will to start making the farm pay, we might make some money and save the situation.'

'That's what your Father says,' Mr Mitchell said.

'We never take payment for the farm stuff,' I denied. 'It's very little and we have many hungry people.'

'Oh, but you'll have to,' he said.

He left it unsaid that Father had taken to drinking heavily, but I knew it. I saw the whole situation in one awful moment and then I heard Mick-Joe talking softly, but still I did not believe it was true.

'We're all to be kept on here,' he said. 'We could earn our keep ... every one of us. We have had a poor farm. It was a hobby of the Master and he made nothing out of it. He let himself leave his affairs get into Queer Street, but we could get that righted ...'

I half heard what Mick-Joe proposed to do.
'We would run cattle on the fields and export
bullocks to Britain. We might start on
fattening pigs. We would certainly improve the
garden and the fowl ... geese, cockerels ...
butter and maybe milk...'
The talking went on and on and at last I
wondered if it could ever be done. Mick-Joe
said that Selina and Marcella and Sally would
be glad to work their fingers to the bone.
'They're country women. They can turn
their hands to anything and glad to do
anything to save the Master.'
He looked at me and maybe he noticed that I
had lost hope.
'You're the Mistress now, Miss Shanne.
You would have to be the heart of it all.
Without you, we could do nothing. Hear this
and understand. There's no escaping our
destiny. See yourself watching a horse
galloping the fields. Doesn't your heart beat
with his? When you see the fox run, don't you
bleed for the courage in his chest? You're Irish
to the backbone and you love and cherish both
sides to every question. Do you know what
that is? Your ancestors were planted here like
any seed out of the ground ... and from out of
the same seed came the shamrock...'
'Father might not have me do it, not the
farm,' I said, but I knew Father cared for
nothing any more.
'He'll let you do what you want to do,' Mr

Mitchell said, and presently he took himself off with a parting shot. 'When did he not give you your way?'

I helped Father to bed and went to sit in the kitchen with Mick-Joe and Marcella and we built castles in the air.

I would still help Father in the dispensary and I did my lessons in every bit of spare time I had. We had decided to get Merton House to its feet and maybe we did it. For the next two years we were never done working. The project caught fire slowly. Eventually we ran cattle in the fields and sold pigs for bacon. We sold butter and eggs in the market at Ballymahon, Mick-Joe and I. The garden flourished. Mick-Joe and I took produce in a dog-cart into Ballymahon Market once a week on Saturdays. We sold butter and eggs and poultry, prepared for the table. We now sold vegetables and fruit instead of giving them away. The top people were angry with us. They thought we had shamed Merton House, for it was not genteel for professional people to take to trade. A doctor's daughter had no place to be bargaining among the hucksters in the market and haggling with the drovers' wives over a pound of butter and half a dozen brown eggs. We were keeping pigs too and there was a new smell about the proud stable-yards of Merton.

'*Miss Shanne's Grandfather, the old, old doctor, God rest him, must be turning in his grave, that his only son had turned into a pig jobber.'*

My favourite time of the day was when I helped in the dispensary. I had closed the memory of Mother up in the fragrance of honeysuckle. I pretended to myself, in a small dream, that Mother had Sally still to help her see to the fern in the sitting-room. Yet the fern was unhappy. It shed its leaves like tears and made me sad.

I told myself that we did make some money. We were able to pay bills at last, in the Ballyboy shops and in Ballymahon town. Mick-Joe did a small milk round. Once a week, the people settled their books.

I could not shut my eyes to the fact that many people did not visit at Merton any more. There were old friends, who crossed the street to avoid me and looked the other way. Twice a week, I went to Miss Byrnes's house for tea and listened to lectures on Red Cross and home nursing.

The turn of the year was cold and bitter and dark and wet, yet Miss Byrnes was always kind to me, showed me a soft side I had never known she possessed, praised my work at the classes and set me at the top of the order of rank. There were girls who came to these lectures, who were among my friends, who had deserted me in friendship. Miss Byrnes was as constant to the House of Merton as the North Star Pole was to the sailor. God bless her! I could never

realise all the little kindnesses she gave me ...
the good tea, the bit of the chocolate cake with
the walnut on it; most of all, the sweet praise.
'I won't waste time asking this question to
the class. I'll just ask Shanne Gregg and she'll
give us the answer. Maybe she had grown up in
an atmosphere of Aesculapius? She had
medicine bred into her from generations before
her. I have already awarded her the senior
stripe in both the classes ... You can challenge
her for it, if you like, but you'll not vanquish
her.'
The time passed slowly that winter and
maybe I fitted well into the Red Cross and
home nursing. The winter seemed as if it might
go on for ever. The sun might have been lost for
eternity, and perhaps I had grown up at last.
I wore black ankle-length skirts and white
blouses with black-ribboned boaters. I rode
side-saddle in divided skirts on Lady Gay.
Sometimes now, we heard guns in the hills. A
time or two, I came on them in the coverts,
drilling with poles in their hands instead of
rifles, but I knew to do as Mick-Joe had told me
and keep a still tongue in my head about the
'curlews in the hills'. Was I not Miss 'Facing-
Both-Ways'?
I was rolling bandages for Miss Byrnes twice
a week and she never could get enough of them.
There was no further news of the convalescent
home for Screebogue House. I had joined the
Red Cross officially, as something like an

assistant to Miss Byrnes and this was high honour. I might be called to go on a rota for nursing, if a nursing home was ever created. I puzzled over my problem. I was Irish. I was Protestant. The rebels would count me British. Father had fought for Britain in South Africa. Not only was he Protestant, but he was Free-Mason and the rebels could not abide Free-Masons. They were as bad as the Orangemen in the North. Mick-Joe had been Father's batman in South Africa. Mick-Joe was very gloomy about it all. It was possible that Merton House would be burnt over our heads, if a rebellion were to start.

'It's unlikely all the same. Your father's a man with no enemies and he brought half the parish into the world ... and his hand open and generous and his heart kind ... the Master.'

It was tangled beyond disentangling ... mixed up as if life were a kitten with a ball of wool. Mick-Joe had it that the Geraghty family were all rebels, even if Mrs Geraghty did our washing. Bridget was a 'red-hot one' and her motto was 'Ireland for the Irish'. One of these days, he would stick it down her throat for an ungrateful little ragamuffin.

'Maybe she feels the need for shoes on her feet, when the frost sharpens the battlefield of the gate-cottage yard,' I murmured softly...

I had always possessed this way of seeing both sides to a question, and I found it a great disadvantage. I felt sick in heart, that my

51

friends had cold-shouldered me. I felt ill-done by. True I had sold pigs 'crubeens' in Ballymahon Market, but I had no choice if I was to pay Father's debts.

Father provided whiskey bills and they had to be met.

Mick-Joe and I would collect a case of whiskey a week at the grocery off-licence and the hotel bar in Ballyboy. Most nights, he stumbled to bed. There were times when I had to go to the kitchen to seek Mick-Joe's help.

'Don't ever blame him, Miss. He had the heart stole out of his breast when he lost your mother and there is never any finding her again in this world.'

It was coming on to Easter 1916, and there were evenings when Father would let me take on cases that arrived in the dispensary. I knew he had got past trusting himself. Sometimes, he called me by Mother's name.

'Louise. You'll see to it for me, won't you?'

Mick-Joe warned me. 'There are years coming on us, that nobody will believe. Have a true heart to yourself and help the hurt people, as you always did. Just rest easy and wait what's to come.'

He squinted up at me through the red evening sky.

'It's the horses you're fretting about,' I said. 'You're worrying they'll be taken for the battlefields of France.'

'Are your eyes tight shut Miss? Our horses might be taken for the battlefields of Ireland.'

He looked at me for a long minute, as if he wondered what to say to me.

'Isn't the rebellion coming down on our heads this minute? It will be a country with the dogs of war running free and the land of Erin red with blood. There will be people, who should have lived at peace and they at war, one against the other. Ireland will be rent in twain before they're done with it, like the veil of the temple, when our Lord was crucified.'

He wondered whether to tell me what he was going to say next. Then he knew he could trust me.

'Maybe you know what I'm going to say, but maybe you don't. There's been a whisper about it. Lieut Col Toby Phillips has given Screebogue House to the British Army as a convalescent home for British Army officers. I expect they will be Irish boys mostly, but one thing is sure. Miss Byrnes will rely on your help there, and you'll have to give it, and that's for Britain—and for your own Mr Dermot, God rest his soul.'

So the news was out at last. Screebogue House was our nearest neighbour north across the turbary. It was safer to take a horse and ride the long way along the road. The bog holes were reputed to go down to the centre of the earth. It was not worth chancing it for the mile it saved.

Toby and Caroline Phillips had lost two sons in Flanders, twin sons, lost the same moment.

Mick-Joe told me all the details of what had been rumour drifting round the County of Longford. Screebogue House was destroyed with the death of Dermot and Rory. God help me. I mourned for Dermot too, bitterly still.

The stable might lie empty ... the tennis court neglected. No brides would ever come to take the place of 'Herself'. But now the news was out. The offer had been accepted, and plans started. Screebogue House would be equipped as soon as possible. The wounded would move in and the establishment would be supplied from Miss Byrnes's young ladies. Had we not been working to undertake such a task? There were more and more casualties from the battlefields. This was a need they never seemed to be able to fill. We girls would be doing urgent work for the allies.

I rode up to Screebogue one day on Lady Gay. The black retriever might watch for his young masters. His tail had lost its jollity. He moped. He lost his enthusiasm for the gun-room. Sometimes, he whined in apology, but there was none. When Mother had died, they had almost adopted me ... not quite. I remembered the night Aunt Caroline had stayed with me and I had wept into the softness of her bosom, till the day dawned and it was all true. I remembered the way she had dried my tears. I remembered her advice.

'You must find trouble greater than your own, Shanne. You must work from dawn to dusk, so that when you go to bed you sleep. Never look back down the soft loving years, and never think of the years the locust has eaten. Come to us for help. I'd ask you to live with us, but your father would be lost without you.

'There are so many people with big trouble, people this war has destroyed or will by the time they're done with it. You have your little farm now. Make a go of it and good luck to you!'

I told Mrs Geraghty that Mick-Joe had told me about the convalescent home in Screebogue and she looked at me sadly.

'I hope Mistress Caroline doesn't think her two boys Rory and Dermot will be returned to her. I hope that she's not praying for miracles.'

'She has more sense,' I said crossly, but I wondered if she had. 'God have mercy on her!' I said, and she muttered that I had taken to talking like a Catholic.

We were bigoted, of course, at school level. I recalled the battles on all sides between the model school Protestants and the convent schools, to say nothing of the Christian Brothers. We had used grass sods for ammunition. Why should the pups of one litter be set against another litter because of an accident of birth? I recalled the incident, when I pinned the Catholic champion by the ears, to the ground, aged ten. I screeched out to him and was ashamed of it now that 'Roman Catholics went to Mass riding on the Devil's ass.' He spat blood and one tooth into my face, when I let him up.

'Proddy Woddy, stick to the wall. A ha'penny candle will light ye all. Get out of Ireland. It isn't yeers and never was.'

It had happened in Scotland too, this guerilla warfare among children, after years of history and ignorance. Bigotry was a birthright and long memories. There was great religious division and to my mind it did not mean much. I was as Irish as the Catholics. Maybe they had been there first, but if I looked up history it might have counted to three hundred years. The strange thing was that we loved each other. We held each other no true hate. The Geraghtys were my 'patients' and I admired Bridget for the way she kept a brave face in a hard life. I saw to it that Sally took home some food for her and she had my old clothes since I was little, but maybe she held it against me that I went in fine clothes and she was always as if she had been dressed from a scarecrow...

I must think it all out, but now was the time when I must ride to Screebogue. John James, the Screebogue groom had ridden over with a note for me this morning, Aunt Caroline would like me to come to tea. The affairs of the convalescent home were in motion. The place was a hive of industry. It was time I came to have a look at it.

I had got rather short of clothes in the years since Mother's death. Fashion was simple, even if I was counted grown-up. My things were all let down or let out ... a tweed coat in black mourning, a white blouse with a black tie or maybe a black bow ... a straw hat or a boater with ribbon. Just because it was a formal visit to Screebogue, I had worn Mother's riding kit again and her riding bowler with the veil. My outfit had a visible effect on Selina as she saw Mick-Joe put me up in the saddle.

'And your hair as dark as your mother's was, if you ride in along the drive to Screebogue like that, Miss, I hope Caroline Phillips doesn't faint on the front steps. I never saw the like of it. You're your own mother, risen and come back to ride her mare again. Herself will never be dead, while there's life in your body. I don't know how the Master bears the sight of you always in front of his eyes. Isn't it a pity that the whiskey is the only ease for his pain? God knows he drinks us out of house and home, but many a fine man has done the same thing to his family, and it will pass in time. It is an awful thing to see a man destroyed entirely, but 'tis a common story. There is nothing for it, but time to pass, and time moves slow.'

I was a fool to have put on Mother's kit. It was asking for trouble. I went cantering up the long drive of Screebogue to the granite steps and here the groom was waiting and Caroline Phillips was walking slowly down to me. I saw the way both their faces looked at me and Aunt Caroline turned as white as a ghost. John James the groom, took Lady Gay away towards the stables and I went slowly up the steps with Aunt Caroline. She had lost all her plump jolliness. It was strange what total grief did to people. She took my hand in hers and we made a tour of the enormous house that I knew as well as my own. It was a very grand place. It had a tennis court and a croquet lawn ... a spinney with purple violets and white ... a bank of wild strawberries. They had gardeners, who kept the place like the garden of Eden. The two boys, now dead, had been my childhood companions, and one telegram had reduced Aunt Caroline to a pile of ashes. Her spirit revived like turf ashes when I breathed on it. She had stopped on the top landing to look out over the grounds.

'It's going to be happy again, the old house,' she said softly. 'In a kind of way it will bring them home to us again, but there are so many of them, the ones that will come this way from Flanders. It must be a place for healing and for forgetting the hurts of the spirit and the frightfulness of war.'

Blackie was looking down to where men were working on the croquet lawn and Aunt Caroline told him that he would soon be playing tennis again. His tail wagged, as if he understood her.

'Do you remember the ball man?' she asked me. 'When Blackie got tired of fielding for cricket too long, he used to confiscate the ball and take it away for a rest and we would all be mad with him. Poor old Blackie! Poor children, all past now. Maybe it will come again in a sort of miracle but I have no hope of it . . . just other children and other hurt ones.'

The village carpenter, Grogan, was at work on the second floor. There was a section of the ground floor for the family. They had kept the library for themselves and it was to be the dining-room and the estate office. It had a grand open fire and Aunt Caroline looked into it now.

'I shall invite them to take tea with me there. They will toast muffins and tell me all the little things about themselves. It will be just the same, as if my boys had come home from school for the holidays, just the same, yet never the same faces . . . and all that love . . . never again, and poor little Shanne . . . my daughter, who would have been . . . Oh, my darling . . . so young, to know the end of bright love.'

In the hall was a flat separated off and private, two bedrooms, an office with a desk, a cosy sitting-room. There was a name painted on the door.

Matron. Mrs Isobel Love

This was the first I had heard of her and Aunt Caroline explained, deliberately turning her mind off Dermot...

'We have a matron coming, a doctor's widow! Very capable person and a medical background, the same as yourself. She's used to a practice and patients. She has a daughter called "Maggie Love" world famous now. You see her photos in magazines, though she's not twenty yet.'

'Maggie Love,' I echoed in surprise. *The* Maggie Love? I knew the story. The girl who went over to France with a show. Everybody did. She's beautiful and she's talented. London is in uniform. The theatres are playing to packed houses. 'Who loves Maggie Love? We all do.' It jumped at you from every hoarding. The crowds on leave packed her shows. She went up like a top star to shine the Milky Way.

'She is the most beautiful girl you ever saw, Shanne. I met her, when I met Isobel Love to interview her for here. She's only a girl still, but she has something about her ... a perfection. I expect she will come and give us a show here in time.'

I knew one of her songs. I hummed it over to myself.

'I'm for you and you're for me.
I love you and you love me. That's the way
  we'll always be
For ever and ever and ever...'

60

I was intrigued with the idea of having Maggie Love open Screebogue, but it was a presumptuous thought and I quenched it. Like all the girls I foundered on the thought of what I would wear and the cupboard was bare. I was still in mourning. My pretty things were all outgrown. Besides she would have no time for stragaving across the sea to Ireland. I admitted to myself, that I was jealous of her. There seemed very little glamour about the milking shed and the labour of the dawn scene every morning. The eternal bump-thump of the butter, when it did come.

'Come butter, come butter, come butter come,
Every bit as big as my bum.'

Sally Geraghty was a great one for keeping up our spirits.

I would chide her for being common, but I had a suspicion that she might be twice as capable as Maggie Love, who was obviously a chocolate-box beauty, even if she had had the courage to visit the battlefields of France, right up to the front lines. She must have heard the sounds of shell-fire. I had heard the rifle fire in the hills, but I suspected my courage. I was even afraid of cattle stragaving round the fields. The thought of them being herded into wagons at the station put remorse into me (on the way to the slaughter houses in Liverpool

61

over a stormy sea). I wanted to be like Father and stay working in the dispensary, but there was no chance of it. There was a bar against women doctors, but Florence Nightingale had caused a new wind to blow in the Crimea. One day, I knew my dream might come true. Were there not Garret Anderson and Jex Blake? There had always been a Dr Gregg at Merton House. If I had been born a boy, it would have been very simple. They all went to Trinity College to read medicine and in due course returned to Merton and fell in love and married and had children and so it went on ... a dynasty of doctors.

Mother had made the mistake of having me, but once I was there, it was an accomplished fact and Mother had not been good at having babies. She must have no more. I had worked it all out in my head. I had played with the Phillips boys all my life at Screebogue House. We were always together. If I was not at Screebogue, they would be at Merton driving Miss Hinchley wild with the short cuts they took, across the turbary on their way home.

'You boys will never live to grow old,' she threatened them. 'Can't you be warned and take care? If you go on as you're doing, it's dead you'll be and then you'll be sorry for it, when it's too late and you're both lying dead at the bottom of the world in the biggest bog hole ever there was, and duck weed for a burial robe, all tangled in your hair.'

Miss Hinchley had not foreseen the shell that took the two of them in one second, far more deadly than any turbary land in Ireland, but they were gone and my heart was broken for Dermot Phillips. It had always been the understood thing between the two families. One day Dermot and I would be married and live happily ever after. The Phillips family looked on me as their own. It was an accomplished fact, but the best laid schemes of mice and men gang aft agley...

Caroline Phillips put her hand over mine and gripped it.

'It's time I was telling you what's been happening, Shanne. You'll be pleased. Your father is to get the position of M.O. here. It will be very good for him and give him something to do. Since your mother died, he's turned into a dead man. He will like the young soldiers and their attitude to life. It will be good for Toby and me too. We'll be catapulted out of our old ways, out of our sorrows, probably. There's no doubt that these soldiers will take the place into their hands and shake it up a bit. There's another confidence I have for you. There's an assistant being posted to your father, a man who knew Dermot and Rory. He was hit in the same incident and was grievously injured. He saw the boys destroyed between one minute and the next. It was bloody murder that day. They thought he was killed, but he lived to fight another day, by some sort of miracle. I doubt

63

you've heard of him?'

I shook my head and helped myself to another muffin and buttered it and spread it with what I knew was Selina's best bramble jelly.

'The chap is here already. He went down to Merton to meet your father, but I don't know if they met. He's a strange young man . . . a major and not a word to say for himself. You know it's pretty good for Toby and myself to have this forced infusion of new blood. There was a time when I thought it was the end of us here, but now I believe that maybe we'll take up arms again . . .'

She smiled at me.

'Miss Byrnes's young medical ladies are providing staff, so you'll be here. Soon the British Government will stock us up with equipment and then we're all set to go. I know you have no time to spare, but you'll have to make time. The RAMC will be draughting Army nurses to us and they're pretty tough. Now don't refuse to help, Shanne. It's what you joined up for,' she insisted.

'I'll help you,' I said.

'But Shanne, mind what you're saying and to whom. There are families and maybe the same Geraghtys in your gate-lodge above. Maybe they're siding with the rebels for Independence for Ireland. They might be ready to have us all with our throats cut and the houses burned down from about our ears, with the strangers and their cans of paraffin...'

Slowly I had sorted out the curlews on the hills. I had read the slogans tarred on the limestone, and perhaps they dated back to the famine. I had seen the slogans on white front gates, even on our own wrought-iron gates.

UP THE REBELS
WEST BRITAINS GO HOME TO
ENGLAND

At election times, they flourished.

Vote for Dev and free Ireland. Up the rebels. West Britains, go home. Ye're not wanted here.
Vote for O'Keefee and Ireland's dead and will rise and curse you.

We had finished tea in the library and the maid had cleared the tray. Aunt Caroline and I wandered down the front steps again and there was John James with Lady Gay awaiting us. He gave me a lift to the saddle and he was an old, old friend of mine from the days gone by. He told me that his wife had had a son in the night and I congratulated him, asked him the baby's name.

'His name is to be Eamon.'

That was a strange name, I thought, and in another moment, recognised it as De Valera's name.

Oh, God! Were they all secret rebels? In my mind's eye, I saw he daubed letters a foot high in white paint. Maybe John James could be stamped REBEL too, the Geraghtys, the Screebogue groom, even Mick-Joe, but never false to us, never Mick-Joe.

Vote for Dev and free Ireland. Freedom for the Irish after three hundred years of slavery.

Now John James's eldest son had given his life at Mons for the British. His wife had a black armband, but much good it did her. Maybe her tears would wash the white paint away...

Caroline had taken the mare's rein from John James and she said we were going to walk along the drive a bit. I imagined that she did not want old John James to overhear what was said.

I said goodbye to the groom and told him I would ride over to see the baby on the morrow. I had a little knitted coat that would suit him fine, blue for a boy too. My thoughts were like rats caught in a trap. It had been under my eyes and I had not seen it. All my endeavours had been for Merton and its upkeep. There were so many expenses to be met. I would soon be sixteen and time was running up to Eastertide. Selina had gone to mind her old Mother who lived in a flat in Mount Street in Dublin. Tonight, Marcella was cooking the goose and I thought that she'd likely make a hash of it.

Blackie gave a sharp bark at the sight of me and I saw that Uncle Toby Phillips was waiting at the front gate for me.

'I must be off soon,' I said, and leaned to kiss his cheek.

'Marcella is cooking the dinner tonight,' I said. 'I'd best get home soon. Selina is up in Dublin in a flat in Mount Street, looking after her mother. I think I told you.'

'You're a grand lassie,' he said, 'but I think they're all going to cook the goose. You must have seen it coming, little darling, with all the increase in graffiti.'

I did not understand what he meant and he went on.

'The curlews have come down from the hills and out from the marshy places and they're drilled and orderly and seen in the streets now. Soon they'll be fighting and maybe winning. I want you to lie low and say nothing. If there's trouble at Merton, put Mick-Joe on one of the horses and send him to us for help.

'Lie low and say nothing, like Brer Fox,' he continued, 'I know that Mick-Joe is a Geraghty like them all, but he was your father's batman. He'll never hurt him. Lie low and say nothing. They'll not ever forget the time *you* saved the life of the wee lad. No one in that family will ever harm you, but there must be no wild talk out of you. You're a brave child, always have been. God help us to keep faith with faith.'

I knew he had hoped to have me for a daughter-in-law one day, but it was never to be now. 'Confide in your father, Shanne ... in nobody else. God be with us all. It's coming soon now.'

I cantered off along the verge and heard his laugh.

'Don't let Marcella make a hash of the goose, Shanne,' he called. 'We could all go up in the roasting pan.'

There was a broad green verge of grass to the avenue and I turned into it and waved goodbye to Lieut Colonel and Mrs Phillips. Blackie came a little way with me and then he turned back to the gate. I bent over the saddle and sent the grey mare into a gallop and she went as smoothly as the thoroughbred she was. My mind was spinning like a top with all the impossible things. Surely Bridie Geraghty was not a member of the rebels' women's corps, the Cumann-na-mBan? I knew that was what they called it. They were runners and messengers and nurses, but they were rebels against the establishment. The establishment was the police, I knew, and the British soldiers and the people who ran the country. Perhaps I was a West Britain and if so, could I please go home? I knew no other home. I had been born in Ireland sixteen years ago. I sang 'God save the Queen' in Church every Sunday. I was loyal to Britain against the Huns. Ireland was my country too. Always I came back to the same

68

conclusion. I was Miss Facing-Both-Ways.

Here was the gate of Merton House and I knew that my family was of English extraction perhaps three hundred years ago. They had been planted into Ireland from Bristol, people who dealt in the woollen trade. They had prospered and as the years went on, they had aspired to the medical profession.

Mick-Joe had scrubbed the white paint off the ornate gates. He had said very little to me about it, except that it would not happen again. He had been silent about it and very angry.

'Rest tranquil, Miss Shanne. It was a mistake.'

'God, have they no gratitude in their hearts?'

I had to open and close the gates and there was a great silence about the gate-keeper's cottage. I went at full gallop down the hill and wondered if they had all turned against us and wanted us gone? I wished that Selina would come safely home again and her mother better. We were understaffed without Selina, especially with the farm. Mrs Geraghty was probably down in Merton to leave the clean washing and she would be having a good gossip and a fine tea. Together, they would steer Sally and Marcella through the cooking of the goose, God help it! I galloped down the incline of the hay-field at a great pace. I made for the turn of the avenue to where the mossed bank made a fine jump for the hunt, a double bank and a jump that Lady Gay knew well. She

69

braced herself at it. She landed with her front feet placed perfectly and then changed feet like any ballerina and the great leap down again.

There was a man near the bank, his head in his hands, not a sound out of him. Lady Gay shied sideways in a long skittering leap that nearly had me off her back. I recognised the uniform, the snakes of Aesculapius, the RAMC, the Medical Corps. I recognised the major's crown, but he seemed young. Yet war in France was a forcing house. He had not raised his head. I approached the bank with decorum. He had fair silver hair and the head still down on his arms, as if he hid out from life. I dismounted at last and walked over the grass in silence. Then I stretched out my hand and touched the major's crown on his shoulder. He jumped as if I had shot him and I thought that here was a very nervous young man … old in battle. There was only one person he could be. Here was Major Gareth Chandos, my father's assistant. He had been in action with the Phillips twins. He had seen my loved Dermot and his brother destroyed in one flash of fire. A second later, he himself had been blotted out in the collapse of the whole trench. They said he had shell-shock. I knew nothing of him … only that he had survived and the twins were gone for ever.

His eyes sought for mine and his voice was apologetic.

'Maybe you're Mistress Shanne Gregg? I'm

70

looking for Acting Colonel Gregg and I expect that's your father?'

This was the man who had been dead and was alive again. I had had news of him. He was French of Irish descent. This I knew. He had seen Dermot die. I choked on the knowledge and knew that he was well aware of who I was and what Dermot had meant to me. I held his hand too long and wondered how to break his reserve in such circumstances.

'Thank the Lord you've come,' I smiled. 'I'm in an awful domestic tangle. Selina is away and Marcella is responsible for the goose. She's no hand at it and neither am I. For pity's sake, come inside to the house and see what's going on. I'm of the opinion that Marcella is in what she calls "a mag".'

I managed to laugh as if there was nothing wrong with the whole world. Mick-Joe came along the meadow and asked me what I thought I was doing at the double bank and the mare in such a sweat? I was still laughing and not much to laugh at. I was parched for a cup of tea and I proposed that we all go into the kitchen and see how the goose was progressing.

I tossed it off casually and he followed me like a lamb and said nothing.

'I'm Shanne and I'm family. I'm Red Cross nurse too, so I'm "kind of" medical. It's a lonely sort of place here. You don't know how welcome you are. We have a farm here recently and maybe we'll make it pay, but first you'll

71

have to help us cook a goose . . . and don't try to evade duty. You shall have the honour of basting the animal. That's the whole secret . . .

'You're welcome to stay and help us eat it, when Father is back from the rounds.'

Father was very kind to him and we seemed to laugh a great deal. He expected to walk back to Screebogue, but Mick-Joe drove him home in the trap. Gareth Chandos had a strange effect on me. I had laughed all the evening, I who seemed to have forgotten the art of laughter. There had been nothing to laugh about, but the day had come up like sunshine after rain.

Father and I waved the trap off up the avenue and went into the house to wait for Mick-Joe's return. I went out to the stables to help him bed down the mare, for I wanted a talk with him and I wanted it badly. Sally and Marcella had finished clearing the dishes and were toasting their feet at the kitchen fire, so Mick-Joe and I had the privacy of the stables. I blurted it out to him as soon as he led the beast through the door.

'I heard it, but I don't believe it. If it is true, will it be soon? They're planning to rise against Britain, the ones for freedom, aren't they? They call themselves rebels, but we're all friends and brothers and there are so many dead in Flanders, who are Irish boys. Maybe the pride of the nation and no sense in it, to throw such lives away.'

72

'I would not be thinking of it at all Miss Shanne,' he said dourly.

'But is it true at last?' I pursued him. 'For pity's sake, tell me what will happen to us if there's a rebellion.'

He was a relative to the Geraghtys at the gate-lodge. They were all inter-related, down to Eamon, the new-born baby to the Screebogue head-groom.

'They won't hurt us here, Miss. It will soon be all over and only an Easter lily to watch out for, maybe as a kind of memory that they tried again one more time.' He hissed through his teeth as he rubbed the mare down and he spoke no more till he had her rug on.

'It won't reach us here, only what we've had … a shot in the night and marching men … maybe a raid on a house to find arms or ammunition, the tarring of the gates and the walls. Half the "British" soldiers are their relatives or went to school with them. It's the poor are the rebels not the grandees, with their rent money stashed beyond in Britain. It's the curlews in the hills that will take to the rising to get the shoes to put on the childer in the winter and food for their bellies and work for their hands.

'Listen to me, Miss, and listen well. Maybe they're going to call down the whirlwind, but we have no answer to them, not now. The Hun has a grip on our throat and souls are being lost in mud and water. Listen to me and hear what I say to you. It won't reach us here, only what we've had. Our middle class has always been for Britain and for its prosperity, bedded in and comfortable. The shopkeepers have their stocks and share. They won't see the man that pays the piper turned out.'

He gripped my arm and looked at me earnestly.

'Keep a still tongue in your head. Go on here as you've always done. Help the sick people and the ones with nothing. Don't take sides. The curlews whistle high and they've made their army, such as it is. They'll burn up their souls for the freedom of their green land and "Ireland right or wrong". They'll get no thanks from Kaiser Bill, when the battle's lost. Oh, God! Forget what I said. 'Tis no business of yours, Miss Facing-Both-Ways. That's the way you were born and you've chosen to take a stand against Germany with Miss Byrnes and all her young ladies and much good may it do you. But which way will ye turn when ye come to the cross-roads?

'It's hard to know what to do with you for maybe it's a hard row you've chosen to hoe . . . Just do like your father said and learn to heal the sick. You were always a great hand at it and maybe a woman has a gentler way about her than any man. If I were to be asked to see into the future, I'd say that probably women will start carving their own way, but don't rush at it, Miss. Hasten slowly and with kindness in

74

your hands.'

I went to bed and thought it all over. It was probably nonsense. More interesting was the thought of Major Chandos. I must try to get a tender from him for trade . . . butter, eggs, milk, poultry. I could do with business with the convalescent home and I went after it. I found the major in Isobel Love's office, filling in forms and he seemed glad to see me.

Maybe he knew all about me. I imagine he did, but I was a smart businesswoman. I wasted no time, just told him honestly that I was after trade with him. I wanted to sell farm produce and I wanted to provision the home and I was an honest woman. Two years ago I had been thrown in to sink or swim. I survived. I found that if you work hard, you can make money and I had been in debt. I had learned how to pay off debts and I made a great many friends . . . perhaps lost as many too. I very much wanted to get the tender to provision Screebogue Convalescent Home.

He saw I was ashamed and was sorry for me. Caroline Phillips came in and laughed me to scorn.

'Shanne, my pretty one. Of course, you'll get the tender for the home . . . butter, milk, eggs and poultry. Good luck to you! We know we can trust you and you can trust us. It was no easy thing you did to turn to the farm and it's gone like a rocket and your affairs are getting straight, but don't forget Miss Byrnes. You're

75

a Red Cross nurse now, we'll want you on the rota, I don't know how you'll find the time, but find it you must. You're our right-hand girl here too. It may be a little time before the equipment is moved in, but there's a back-log. One of these days the consignment of gear will arrive, and then maybe Miss Byrnes will send you off as an outrider to call up all the Red Cross personnel. These things always happen without warning. One morning we'll have a signal from the War Office and the next the lorries will be rolling. Then maybe you'll be riding like Paul Revere to call the girls to the service of their country. Isn't it exciting?'

Aunt Caroline made short work of the contract for provisioning.

'If they close the door to you, Shanne, they close it to Screebogue. It's yours. Think no more about it.'

That was that, in Longford, but Major Chandos was embarrassed for me. Caroline Phillips had an idea that the rebellion would never come. The struggle had been going on for 300 years, maybe 600 years, but it had come to nothing. We had been planted into Irish land, and surely by now we had rooted. The ridiculous thing was that there were so many Irish out in France fighting the Germans ... good British tommies as British as the British themselves. 'IRELAND FOR THE IRISH' screamed the white paint on the walls. There had been a letter from Selina in that day.

'Her mother was better. She herself would be home to us soon. She missed us very much. She would haste home like the wind. There was a great uneasiness in the city. The tempest was blowing and we must all shelter before the blast to survive. The corn can rise again, when the storm is past. The Catholic childer were educated about Cromwell and King Billy, but it was all a long time ago. The Irish could hardly win now and it might be an awful 'shennanigan' about nothing, but Dublin was in a right turmoil. She herself hadn't got a wink of sleep with the guns and bombs blasting off. It was even harder to get out of the city. She was going to try to sneak out by Broadstone, the way the train went and get a lift to Longford in a horse and cart. If she didn't get home soon, she'd go daft with worry about the family. She had heard that they were burning the big houses in the country and wasn't it a crying shame? God would keep us all safe till she was home to us again and might Mary, Queen of Heaven, keep me safe under her blue robe for the mad way I was riding Lady Gay round the country, as if I had taken leave of my senses. If I was to have an accident and go to join my sainted mother in heaven, what would I say to the poor mistress that I went off and left ye all alone and nobody to look after ye? Take care now. I saw a dead man in the street today ... a Dublin Constabulary man, shot through the head and *in the gutter and nobody even looking at him and I thought that it was a terrible thing that there was nobody to go to his help or care for him. Is it savages we're becoming to leave a man lying in the gutter and his life's blood running free down the drain and no priest near by, with the act of contrition, that might steer him to paradise?'*

Aunt Caroline was the lady of County society. She had the idea that rebellion was all politics that had been going on for hundreds of years, since the Battle of the Boyne. It had never come to anything. We had been planted into the Irish and we had become more Irish than the Irish themselves. The Catholic children had been educated to hate Cromwell and William of Orange, but the Protestants skated round history. 300 years had gone by, maybe 600 at that and still the British had not been thrown out. They had colonised Ireland, thought they had civilised it. Three hundred years was a long rule ... enough to be established ... enough to establish the British way of life. Now there was going to be one of these periodic uprisings or so it seemed and I knew well that I wanted no part of rebellion.

The history of the Siege of Limerick was a blank part in my history book. Bridie Geraghty had painted it in child's poster paints. At any rate, I knew that an Irish rebellion would be disastrous in the middle of one of the most vicious of 'the Foreign Wars'. I was well aware that the flower of Britain, straight from school was being butchered in the French trenches. The schoolboys I knew had no life expectancy in modern trench warfare. They lived in squalor in the filth of the land they called 'trenches'. They shared quarters with the rats and the lice and still they could sing songs. They were the bravest of the brave, but for what purpose? 'In the going down of the sun and in the morning, we would remember them'. Somebody was to say that. They were on our conscience.

Another letter arrived from Selina. At any moment, she might be walking 'in the back door'.

'IRELAND FOR THE IRISH' screamed out the limestone walls. I tossed in nightmares against my pillows, but Selina still did not come. Maybe she had been lost in the planes of Broadstone station?

'Her mother was game-ball now and able to see after herself. The city was in a great state of uneasiness. There was big trouble. The police were searching the trams for guns even at Nelson's Pillar, but young girls would take guns from the boys and shove them down the front of their blouses and cower into the black shawls. When she came home, she'd tell us all, but it was her opinion that Dublin would be entirely destroyed.'

Each evening, Father and I sat over dinner

and Father finished his decanter of port. Then he took to the topaz whiskey as a sure anodyne for pain. Towards bedtime, he left the dispensary to me ... There came strange late calls in the evenings. I had no right to take the responsibility and I knew it. I recall one evening when another man crawled to the sitting-room window and scratched at the pane. Father was asleep and did not hear but I went over and opened it.

'I have a bit of a cut with a scythe, Miss Shanne. Would you have the grace to bind it up for me?'

'Hush!'

There did not seem to be much need for secrecy, but I went along with it. I knew by now what the drill was: '*Bind the cut up tight and let the bird go free.*'

It all seemed very easy, but there was a long time, till the stain was pink enough, and well I recognised a gun-shot wound. I asked him straight out.

'Is the rebellion started at last?' I said. 'Are the curlews down from the hills?'

'The pass-word is to yourself, Miss Shanne. Let the bird go free. Curlews is wild birds and when you treat a wild bird, you open your hand and leave him, where you find him.'

There were more of these patients in the night hours and I did what I could. I would not turn them away. I bound up what could only be gunfire, injuries dealt in battle, out in the darkness of the night. Father should have shouldered the burden. Instead he left it to me and I did the best I could and always I let the bird go free … left it where I found it.

I knew I was walking perilous ground but always in my head ran the words … *MY COUNTRY RIGHT OR WRONG.* Why should I take the side of the enemy? I had been born in Ireland and my people there down so many years. If I went to a Protestant church and sang God save the King every Sunday, that did not make me a Protestant woman, who sinned with each breath she drew. I had as much right to the reflex of Killarney as the next man. Ireland was mine.

The Red Cross was just an accident. I had wanted to learn more about healing the sick and I had joined up for something to do. It did not mean I wanted Britain to conquer the whole world. Ireland was mine. I was almost sure of it … but I didn't know the first thing about it. Perhaps I was as much a rebel as the brave Bridie Geraghty, who had a desire to walk in whole boots, when the snow lay on the ground and icicles hung by the wall and Dick, the shepherd blew his nail, but it was all a great puzzlement to me. Most important of all to me was the new officer at Screebogue.

Major Chandos used Mrs Love's office for the paperwork he had to do. There were lists of all the commodities that were in transit to us, supplies of everything under the sun. He had to search for errors or omissions. One day sooner or later lorries would start to roll in and it would take the hardest work we could do to make Screebogue a paradise for wounded young soldiers. The house itself must be for convalescence and no money had been spared. It was one of the stately homes of Ireland and now it had a destiny to fulfil. These young men had maybe been spoilt by life, before they discovered 'trench warfare', this new horror, where life was reduced to hate, day after day . . . and the gladiators dug in, face to face and one lived or died in water and cold and mud and death. They must have found it hard that lice was just another common factor and that dysentery inhabited every man's bowels. It was quite impossible to come to terms with 'trench warfare'. Chandos had been a casualty at the same moment or a split second later than the Phillips twins, it had happened at the start. He was a man with a precious heritage. The shell had brought down fifty yards of fresh tunnelling, destroyed it into pieces of what had been whole men a moment before. It had seemed a long time till they got him out. The twins had been blasted at his shoulder . . . his own company. He was not expected to survive, but he did. They diagnosed it as 'shell shock' and that was it. Then, two years later, the commander-in-chief had heard about the set-up of Screebogue and knew the parents of Rory and Dermot. It was he who made the

War Office give Chandos his chance of survival and even he thought it was a long shot.

'Far better to send Chandos back to his vineyards than keep him to cruelty and reality. The Phillips boys were his good companions. Yet this place is a niche for him. He can go as assistant to the local GP who will be the officer in charge, with the temporary rank of colonel.'

And that was my father. I had tried once or twice to ask Father about these men who came for help in the surgery, but he told me to leave politics alone. It was none of my business. I was only a child yet.

'Play about with the surgery the way you always liked to do and see to the household. You have done well. If Sally Geraghty has no stomach for cleaning up blood for her own countrymen, do it yourself, but don't talk about it to a soul. It's nobody's business if a farm labourer gets the cut of a scythe and don't take the chance of telling the whole parish about your great aptitude to stop bleeding.' He recalled and regretted his severity to me.

Then he went over to the whiskey bottle and poured out a very amber half tumbler and took it down neat.

'That will be my ration for tonight, Shanne. The stuff makes me forget my own wits, but there are times when a man *must* forget.'

He was as good as his word and we had a pleasant evening and no man came scratching at the lit window. It was Easter Monday the next day and we sat long over breakfast, till the dog in the back yard barked a visitor. I wondered who would be coming on a visit and went to the window to look and there was Miss Byrnes mounted on her safety bicycle, coming at speed down the avenue to the front door. She had reached the damson-tree corner and she was dressed in her Red Cross uniform. Her divided skirt was neat and trim and her official badge was clear to see in the bright air. 'The Red Cross' meant the care of the sick and the wounded. It meant neutrality in time of war, no matter what I thought to myself now. I did not even know what I thought now. It might not differentiate between curlews and rebels and British tommies from Flanders and maybe officers were different to men from the ranks. They had a 'commission' so I thought. It might have some difference. It seemed to me that I had a fearful ignorance of all things both military and political.

Miss Byrnes was a fanatic about the Red Cross. I used to think that she had too much money and too little to do. It was a great pity that she had no husband. She would have made a wonderful wife. She was splendid at organisation. Last month she had produced an ambulance for Screebogue Convalescent Home by dint of buying O'Toole's the baker's van and sewing two red crosses on its canvas-covered wagon sides.

'The Red Cross has as much power as the crucifix has to Christians,' she had lectured to us in her severe voice. 'The Red Cross gives passage to wounded and safety against all evil.'

For no reason I had said 'like the three wise monkeys' which had raised such jollity in the class, that I had been sent home to discipline me for frivolity ... but that had been a few weeks ago ... or had seemed so, yet it was only the week running up to Easter Sunday.

At any rate, Miss Byrnes had not used the ambulance this time. I did not feel too happy about the old work-horse, for he had delivered bread for twenty years and he tended to stop at intervals. He might not take kindly to enemy fire. Marengo might be a better choice, but once he was started, he might be hard to stop. I felt very depressed about the whole thing and knew I was not confident enough. This morning, the black dog sat on my shoulder and all my joy ran like sand through my fingers. It had all quite gone, the happiness and the joy that had been Merton House before Mother's death. All the problems today seemed to be rising up the horizon in black indigo bars. The brightness was fading from the morning.

Sally had gone to open the door to Miss Byrnes and I was glad to see her apron spotlessly clean. I felt oddly cheered. At least I knew I did not *look* depressed, yet well I knew the black dog was close by.

'Good morning, Miss Byrnes,' Sally said. 'What brings you so early? The Master and Miss Shanne are still over breakfast. They'll be cheered to see you. Come on inside, while I run and fetch you a fresh pot of tea and some new buttered toast.'

We listened to Miss Byrnes as soon as we had made her welcome.

'It's a disaster,' she said. 'The Green Howards were not expected at Screebogue for two weeks. Matron is due before then. The stuff has arrived, but it is all lying about ... beds not made up—wards not polished. Nothing's ready except the croquet lawn. What good is that for men just invalided out? We've had a retreat across the Channel. The War Office is expecting fresh-wounded, indentured for this area in Ireland. We are to prepare to receive them more or less at once ... They are in transit from France this minute.'

Her voice sank to a whisper.

'The rising in Ireland started in the night. That's the red alert. There were rumours long-foretold of a rising against the Crown. So, it's started in the night, the rebellion at last. There were columns of rebels, trained soldiers, marching on Dublin, through Leinster, Munster and Connaught, all through the darkness. The British troops are under direct rebel attack this morning. They say that Dublin is burning and the smell of its burning is stretching half across the country. There is blood running in the streets and British soldiers and DMP men being gunned down.

'The Irish people don't know it yet. Fairy House Races is on today. It's a high day and a holiday. If people have any choice, it's to the Races they'll go. It's my belief you'll have precious few races, in the future. There's trouble coming down in Ireland, like she hasn't had for a long time.'

Miss Byrnes caught my shoulder and shook it.

'Our officers from France should arrive today, but Dublin is trouble for them now ... likely be roundabouted down to The Curragh. I've given you a list of the roll-call for Screebogue Home Red Cross. With luck, patients might arrive in convoy before the sun goes down. I want you to round up all the girls in their homes. I want them all at Screebogue House to have it ready. There is no time left. The War Office people have sent the tools. We have to get that home ready within an inch of its life. It must be ready to accept patients, wounded men from France, before the ambulances turn up Screebogue drive. You're the right girl for this, Shanne. You have it in you.'

'Bring her Marengo with her mother's saddle on, Mick-Joe, he will look after her for us,' said Father. 'Lady Gay's too old now.'

I like to think that Father put me up in the side-saddle on Marengo, his own horse.

Then Miss Byrnes again—'*Confirmed red alert for you all. You know the country, but go by the secret ways. Tell each girl to report at once in full kit, ready to start at once, this*

87

Easter Monday.'

'Tis half the county of Longford she must cover by every rough track and hidden way,' Mick-Joe had said under his breath.

Yes, I thought and half of the girls were not talking to me, because I had taken to trade. I had to flush Longford's gentry out of its big houses. I had to persuade them to rise as fast as they could and get the wheels spinning before darkness. Probably there would be a great arguing with parents. It was a labour of Hercules.

Yet my father had looked up at me and kissed my cheek.

'Louise will never be dead, while you live,' he said.

Sally Geraghty had helped me into Mother's riding kit and into the riding hat veiled to my face. People would remember that dread funereal day. I went up the drive like an arrow from a bow. Mrs Geraghty had the gates standing open and I went through with her blessings on my head. Mrs Geraghty was filled with the high spirits of all Irish folk, in times of disaster. Now maybe the rebellion might succeed and Ireland have its own government and shoes for the children's feet in winter.

I cantered by by-ways and back ways, by little wild hills and across the moorland turbary. Sally had stood at my stirrup just before I left.

'Selina will soon be home again, Miss. I want

88

to make your mind easy. I had a note on a bit of torn exercise book early morning. Mick-Joe brought it from his brother, the smith. Dublin is burning like hell-fire and the women have taken to looting the shops. Selina has a shawl, black round her shoulders and she will come on foot through the lines and then try to get a lift on a train. Don't have any fears for her ... and God keep yourself safe.'

It all went round in circles. I had the roster of names printed by Miss Byrnes with a John Bull outfit. She had also written a little note to me with the latest signal from Dublin. I had thought it all a dream, but now I woke up.

'This is no false alarm, Shanne. Take it as real. It's top priority, so do your utmost to make good speed and keep out of sight.'

I was dismayed when the first person I met was Miss Byrnes's brother James. He had been stopped by a detachment of men in strange green uniforms and he on his way to Ballymahon in his trap.

They advised him to go home. It was no use to try to get to Ballymahon, sir. It might be Easter Monday, but there would be no market today. The roads were not safe, so he advised to go home. James Byrnes was well aware of my mission and he worried about me.

'If you are going on this daft trip, and my sister is a fool to risk your life doing it, for pity's sake, keep to the woods and the bosky coverts. The same girls have not treated yourself too kindly. I'd see them in hell if I were you. You're worth the whole pack of them, stuck-up fools playing at being nurses. I'd sooner be nursed by an army mule.'

This was strong talk from James Byrnes, who was a mild agreeable man ...

I went on with it, by every gully and path I could find. Marengo behaved himself like the grand gentleman he was. I paused at this house and then another, but it was a long list. If I stopped by anybody, I was on my way to do some shopping. I got by. They knew Marengo and they said I was a brave lady to put a saddle on him. A few of the old women thought I was my dead mother, God rest her soul!

'You frit the wits out of me, with the look you have of her. Mind how you go now on that baste, for he has a trick of turning to take a bite out of your knee and it's not safe out today, if you have far to go.'

There was an excitement that lived in people's eyes. The rising was on the way. The news was in everybody's mouth. There was a chance that, come winter, there might be shoes for the childers' feet and coats for their backs. Glory be to God! The waiting had been long.

I did not stay more than a few minutes in the big houses, but it took me a while to make them believe that what I said was true. I cantered in by the back avenues, after a few times of having the front door shut in my face. Did I not know that I was not being received by Herself, since I had took to trade in Ballymahon Market?

'The family won't let you see Miss Miranda no longer and if you still stick to Miss Byrnes's Red Cross and home nursing, there will be nobody going to this fine convalescent home, no matter how grand they think Screebogue may be.'

I felt my face redden with such talk and then I noticed Miss Miranda listening, eavesdropping at the turn of the staircase.

'If I don't help, there will be nobody who will,' I said. 'Miss Byrnes will see to it that some of them have the courage. Miss Miranda will be ashamed to have missed St Crispin's Day. She'll know that she will have lost big honour.'

I smiled at the parlour maid and said it was a great pity and was up in the saddle and off down the avenue and away. Maybe Miss Byrnes and I might have to run the home ourselves, I thought, but I knew it was not likely. Most of the girls did what they pleased and I knew it. The snob value of Screebogue House ranked high. Besides, I knew that Miss Byrnes always had other irons in the fire. She had influence with the Richmond Hospital in Dublin and she could dip into the Army Nursing Force too. Even as I closed the back gate at Miranda's mansion, I saw her racing hell-for-leather after me in pursuit, but we soon left her steed far behind. That was to be the pattern of the operation and news had galloped before me soon. Some of them were even ready and waiting for me to come at a cross-roads in a lonely nut grove, and through the day maybe I collected a volunteer force. Still, the time dragged out towards twilight. Last of all, I collected Joanne Webb from Castle Knox and she was one of my good friends still. She had her horse ready and the head-groom had been called to help. He was one of the old ex-servicemen, and his blood was stirring again. He had had the Castle Knox kitchen lay on rations for us and had strapped two ground-sheets ready for use. There was going to be rain he said. Joanne and I must be equipped against the weather. We were old campaigners now, ourselves, 'Danny Mac' said.

'Mind how ye go, Miss Shanne. You'll have picked up the news that's sweeping down the country like a storm. We've been forbidden by the Master to ride out with the pair of ye, but ye know what's come about in the night that's gone. God keep ye both safe from all harm. The minute the sky opens, put the ground-sheets well about ye. It will save ye the worst of it.' (I didn't know then that maybe the ground-sheets might have cost us our lives.)

We rode shoulder to shoulder for a few miles and, after a while, it began to rain and we were very glad of the ground-sheets from the Castle Knox stables. The horses could do with a rest so we sheltered. We had still a part of the roster to finish and there was work still to be done by

92

the time we had almost come to the finish. We had worked our way back near enough to Screebogue, and Marengo and I had had enough. I was glad to come to the rise to the big house. Joanne wished that the rain would go to hell and, just to spite her, it really started to come down hard. I suggested that we by-pass the double bank, but Joanne, of course was not going to take the sensible way round and grinned at me with a wrinkling of her nose as a 'coward' challenge.

I set Marengo at the bank and the next second I heard a shout of 'Halt or I fire', and the Gaelic brogue too—with the softness of green moss.

It was my first sight of fighting men. I had Marengo's front feet on the bank and Joanne was still level with me. We were like a pair of circus riders. We kept time like girls in a chorus line, but all I could think of was the fact that I carried confidential documents that Miss Byrnes had told me to guard with my life. I had lifted Marengo's front feet to the top of the bank ... changed feet and was down the far side. I saw the line of faces below and was over their heads and then off the other side and Joanne level still. There was a buzz of bees that sung about our ears, then a voice,

'Hold your fire, lads. It's only two of the hunt girls.'

I saw the odd makeshift uniforms ... republican kit. We dug our heels into the horses' flanks and lay flat down and went as fast as we could go, and there was no further shooting. It was maybe a mile to the steps of Screebogue and the gate lodge was deserted and the front gate latched. I jumped down and shot the bar, swung the gate wide and Joanne had ridden ahead of me and was half way to Mick-Joe, where he waited at the bottom of the climb to the palladian steps. He was put out with me because Joanne had got home first. I was the one who had started first, God help him! Poor Mick-Joe could never abide it if I were bettered in a fair race. I arrived to hear Joanne take the rough of his tongue.

'I thought ye had more sense than to go riding through an ambush that was laid special for the RIC,' he said. 'Ye're lucky not to have seen yerselves both shot dead, for ye asked for it. Those Republican soldiers are well trained in the arts of guerilla fighting. Don't think it was cleverality that kept the hearts beating in your breasts. They saw ye for what ye were ... two young girls, with no sense. It was God's will that ye were not killed outright this soft spring evening.'

He was not angry after all. I saw it when I arrived at the rise of the steps. He was like a mother whose child has been almost run over on the road, but he was as proud as Punch.

'You've mobilised the troops and we haven't even had the convoy yet. They'll come in their own time and don't be disappointed if they're a few days late. There is terrible confusion up and down the land, but we're staffed now and we'll soon settle in. Major Chandos wants you to see him in Mrs Love's office. She's days overdue now, when she should be in charge. There's been no signal from her ... she's a nice example to everybody.'

He turned and went off towards the stable with the two horses. Joanne went with him. It seemed that Major Chandos had been watching the ambush from Mrs Love's office. I took in the scene in front of Screebogue and could not believe it. Somehow a vast supply of equipment had been dumped down, scattered in precise order, in what looked like every available space. There were Red Cross and VAD girls in regulation kit. They had left their coats and cloaks flung down on the seats along the edge of the grass and were working at shifting the supplies. Their blancoed shoes were twinkling in the fading light and the first stars were showing in a violet sky.

I picked my way up the paraphernalia of battle and nursing equipment ... walking sticks, crutches, sheets and towels, trays and tray-cloths. I knew nothing about the working of such things and I could not have envisaged Screebogue in this orderly disruption. There were so many people all busily at work and with no time to waste and some of the grooms were fixing lanterns along the foot of the climb and in lines regularly every twelve feet or so.

There was so much order and disorder as well. I could never see it all being finished.

Major Chandos appeared at the door of what was the office and he was worried. I ran across to him and saw the relief wipe the tension away. In the hall of Mrs Love's office, the gas was alight. He had been signing letters, and heard the shots, and had taken the field-glasses and had the double bank under observation, and now he was looking at my disordered appearance. I caught sight of myself in the big glass on the wall and saw that the gorse and the briars had taken toll of Mother's riding kit. It seemed impossible that I had dared to report for duty looking like a rag picker's child. The riding habit was an important thing—a symbol to me of something precious that was gone now—to become a sort of talisman.

He was a sensitive young man and he was nothing if not perceptive.

He took my shoulders between his hands and leaned down to look at me closely. I scrubbed my face with my handkerchief and brushed my hair with my hands, scuffled my boots against the carpet and knew I was behaving like a child of four. I tried to apologise for not being dressed for parade and he laughed at me and asked me if I did not think I had done well.

I shook my head and watched my colour drain down to smeary splashy muddy again.

Then he produced a khaki handkerchief and had taken a carafe of water from the writing desk. He used it as a swab and, as gently as Mother would have done it, he sponged all the splashes away and told me if there was to be a roll call, he'd promise I'd pass and he thanked me very much. I had virtually provided the company with a most splendid establishment. I imagine he had heard that I had been snubbed by many of the 'West British'. I imagine that he knew I had been hurt and in trouble. I understood that he set out to put it right now and he had the power to do it. Out of the office, we plunged into the gallery on the second floor and at once we were amid the Red Cross nurses. In the darkening evening they were all dressed the same; dramatic white butterfly caps and starched collars and cuffs and blanco in shoes. He looked at me and said he thought I might prefer to change quickly and I knew he had taken in the slur some of the girls had put on me.

He had gone to the trouble of getting his secretary to unpack my kit and get my quarters ready for me. I was up on the second floor ward for six officers and maybe I'd be happier to get on a par with 'West British Military'. I was to rejoin him in his office as soon as I was ready. He wanted to review the order of work and I must accompany him. He would start things the way they would go on. He laughed at me and invited me to see the funny side of it.

'Mick-Joe would have known better,' he smiled. 'They'll find they backed the wrong horse.'

He was most careful to give me approval and he made no secret of it. He set me in the sky that day and he gave me a star on my shoulder and it was nothing tangible ... only that I had a higher rank and they were all under me and I was a Commandant—first class. I think he made it up himself, and that was how it was going to be, and that was how it was, and I was happy for the first time in the days since I had ridden the back way home from the graveyard with Mick-Joe trying to guide my steps along the safest path for the rough weather that was coming up our sky.

PART TWO

THE SCREEBOGUE CONVALESCENT HOME FOR OFFICERS

When I came downstairs in fresh kit with my shoes blancoed white as any of their shoes, and tucked cuffs, white to match, Crusader's Cross on my apron, it seemed that there were nurses everywhere. There were the Red Cross and the VADs,' who were Miss Byrnes's concern. There were two senior sisters ... professional, trained, on loan to us from the Richmond, Whitworth and Hardwick Hospital in Dublin, who wore a dark blue veil and a navy uniform and had a terrible authority. As yet the matron had not arrived. She was overdue and, somehow, she had been lost in transit in a country at war.

Looking back now at Easter Week, I experienced disorientation. I fail to match day to day. My world is jumbled. I am quite unsure of time. We tried to pack too much action into the normal timing of a day. We could not allot twenty four hours to go twice round the face of a clock. It caused strange things to happen to our memories. Father said it was normal. Given a good rest, we would think normally again. Just for now, we lived between the pages of *Alice in Wonderland*.

The first day was the day I rode Marengo to Screebogue and picked up Joanne Webb from Castle Knox.

The second day was when Bridie Geraghty sang my song and that was important. The third day, I had shipped the cattle and had let the red bullock run free. He had been called 'Dermot' after my Dermot. The real Dermot had become a sweet sad memory ... a boy, who had gone straight to war in Flanders from the sixth form at school. It was sweet and right to die for country ... 'dulce et decorum est'. I had believed it. I had given no thought, as to whether it was or not. It was 'the done thing'. I recalled the impatience of the twins to be gone, afraid that the war would be over too soon. I remembered the day at the station. They had not even looked back as they went. There were times I wondered how the twins had encountered reality. It was like Father Christmas all over again ... a great confidence trick. It was a part of my life I slammed shut. How could two boys quit the lovely graceful life ... co-heirs to a house like Screebogue? I drew a curtain over the reality and the end of it.

When was it when the convoy arrived? At least the home was all ready for them, but it may have been the fourth or the fifth day. For all I remember, Easter Week may have been drawing to an end. I can only remember that the Republican prisoners were taken as rebels. That was certain ... not as prisoners of war. They were not received with honour and with pride, not by the majority of Dublin citizens. All these people were laying down their lives, just as the casualties in France had made the supreme sacrifice. It seemed to be all wrong. Maybe they were soldiers of the same blood, but then I was West British. It horrified me to hear that the Republican soldiers would not be treated as prisoners of war. It was my first big awakening to the situation that existed in Ireland.

I remember the day we moved in the furniture to our ward. We were all at the task and I studied the name boards in the galleries and it must have been one of the early days.

CONVALESCENT HOME FOR OFFICERS AT
SCREEBOGUE HOUSE
LONGFORD
MATRON: MRS ISOBEL LOVE :: OUT:

There was a moveable slot and an :: IN :: that you could change for : OUT : It was all very convenient and I hoped that she would soon come.

There were six wards on the two floors. I tried to get my bearings.

DAY SISTER: GERALDINE FITZGERALD
NIGHT SISTER: MARY SULLIVAN

The sisters were on loan from Richmond, Whitworth and Hardwick. We had started to move the furniture and the bedding up the long haul of the steps and inevitably the teams of nurses had started competition. The nurses were either VADs or Red Cross. I could not understand how it all worked. The wardsmaids were recruited from the maids from Merton and Screebogue. I picked up facts hungrily ... six beds in each ward. Three day nurses and one night nurse. Joanne and a VAD called Honor Purser and I were on Ward three with six beds. We began to assemble the beds and after a struggle found the art. We knew the hospital corners to the sheets. We were accustomed to the red blankets and the Scots plaid rugs and the fleecy mats between the beds. There was an awful lot of work. The floors were for waxing and the windows for polishing. It had all to be done ... The mats between the beds, the carafes of fresh water, the cubicle curtains, the smell of carbolic, the subdued hum of activity, the growth of authority, the foundations of a home far from home. Each ward spied its neighbour jealously and we worked flat out. The sisters were like sheepdogs, who watched every move we made, and the convoy not even here yet. We did not know when it would come. In the meantime, would somebody who understands gramophones take on the task of seeing they were in order? One of the VADs had just dropped a tray of gramophone records on Ward six. It was a shame-making catastrophe, but Lieut Col - Phillips had taken the unfortunate girl down to the library and told her she could choose as many records as she liked. We went from one crisis to another. The wards hummed with the war songs. The fires were all burning brightly back-to-back and the home fires were burning and it was a long long way to Tipperary. I was arranging the little tins of biscuits and the books ... Sherlock Holmes and Sapper ... copies of the *Gem* and the *Magnet*, with Bob Cherry and Harry Wharton. This was a generation that was not to be forgotten. The linen was coming up in a lift for the hot air cupboard. I had to arrange the drug cupboard and see that Sister Sullivan was given the key for her night desk. She greeted me when I brought it to her, looked at her roster and conferred 'Paul Revere' on me because of my ride. She chatted for a while about the state of Dublin City.

'We were glad to get leave to the country. It's been a bit noisy and the streets are full of people with no sense. Wouldn't you think that people would be wise enough to stay in, but the green white and gold flag is flying and Sackville Street has most of its windows shattered and we have to mind the King's soldiers for him. I daresay you girls think it's a great adventure. Now "Paul Revere" you mind how you go! Play fair with me, and I'll play fair with you. We're all born in Ireland, but we're non-belligerent. We're not political creatures and we should not have to walk in danger. Your parents won't thank us if we got you shot for your pains.'

We worked hard all through the night and the place was taking shape, as if the wards grew stage sets. I saw Aunt Caroline Phillips now and again through the night hours, always helping to encourage the very tired girls. It struck me that she had come to realise the extent of the gift the family had given and I put the thought into one idea. There were going to be no more Christmas stockings to be filled ever. There was to be no line of sons. It was the same for me and she put her arms round me once and hugged me against her breast and the tears ran down both our faces, as if they might run for ever. Then we put our weeping aside as a luxury that must be reserved for the silent hours of the nights to come.

Sister Sullivan had a chat with me about the duty I had to help with Merton House.

'We'll arrange set hours for this and you're not to worry about it "Paul Revere". You've had a sad life and greater responsibilities at an early age. We'll all help as much as we can. You've done well to hold the farm for two years. There will be difficulty in your getting off at five in the mornings and riding home, but don't try to put a quart into a pint pot. It won't fit. I'll tell you confidentially that Sister Fitzgerald and I are both farmer's daughters. We were picked because of that. Some person had the choice and it's no secret that it was the

major who seems to run everything here ...
Major Chandos. He joked about it one day,
said he hoped that Sister Fitzgerald and I
might like to try our hands with the milking an
odd time. There's a laugh for you, only it isn't a
laugh. That young man is very attracted to
you.'

She smiled at me and told me to get on with
the good work and it was coming towards the
dawn and the wards were ready. I remember
the way, when we pulled the blinds, the sun
struck the sundial with its first ray and I
thought of the way Christmas would come ...
and no stockings to fill, not any more, not ever.

The convalescent home must prove
something. I could not think what. There
would be no line of sons ... maybe nothing for
any of us. But there must be. There was always
another day and here it was.

Lieut Col Phillips had not been idle. They
had taken advantage of the lights that drilled
the front steps like troops. There was enough
illumination to use the garden to advantage.
They had harvested spring. It was a good time
of the year and a splendid garden to reap.
Beauty lay waiting in the shrubberies and the
herbaceous borders. Lilac bushes were heavy
with blossom ... mock-orange blossom, sticky
budded chestnut with young green leaves,
forsythia, hazel catkins, hyacinths. It was
fitting that they had gone collecting tribute by
moonlight for two sons, maybe for a whole

generation, who had made the sacrifice. They had turned the house into a display of flowers. They were just moving in on our ward and their helpers with them. We had missed what had been happening in the galleries. We had missed the change in the miraculous transformation of the whole big house. There was a rush round form one ward to another and we left the arrangements to the experts. We had been asleep on our feet, but now we were jubilant. There was an atmosphere of exhilaration that made us drunk with sheer joy. Girls, who had curled up like kittens in comfortable armchairs and fallen asleep, woke up dazed with exhaustion and sparkled with sheer excitement. The wards had been precision and comfort and perfection and now was added welcome and warmth and home ... a great thanksgiving for Easter and resurrection.

It was Bridie Geraghty who stole the starlight. I knew vaguely the significance of the Easter Lily. It was to become the emblem of the fight for freedom for Ireland. It was to be known all over the world as the cross the freedom-fighters carried and died for. We had our differences. The Protestants wore the Flanders poppies. It was the same in the days of school with the 'wars' that used to be fought on the way to and from school and maybe small harm in them. The Easter Lily was favoured by the Convents and the Christian Brothers, but it was not clear-cut. There were

Protestants who followed the Easter rising and died for it too. There were as many Catholics fighting for Britain and the King. It was never a clear-cut line and nobody who is not Irish will ever understand it. I know I will never understand it myself. I will never forget the way Bridie presented the straw cross that day with the one perfect lily in the tall cut-glass bowl and the green against its sheath. The colonel helped Bridie lift it to the window that overlooked the full spread of the lawn. Aunt Caroline went over and kissed Bridie's cheek, her eyes bright with tears. It was then we saw the three Flanders poppies, that clustered in a soft bed of shamrock at the base of the arrangement. Bridie was wearing her wardsmaid's uniform and she was as smart as paint. Gone were the poor clothes and the bare feet. She had a crisp cotton dress in pink-and-white and epasulettes on her shoulders and the same long green eyes that I remembered down all the years.

Here was Bridie, near-grown, and here, maybe she had presented the solution to Ireland? Was this the answer to the problem that had existed for so many years? In my mind I thought I had the solution and then lost the secret again. There had been a murmur on everybody's tongue of half-disapproval . . . and somebody laughed and there was a stir through the galleries. The staff all stood to attention and there was silence for a full long minute.

Then Aunt Caroline smiled at us and stretched out her arms.

'Now thank we all our God,' she said. 'I think it might be fitting if we were to sing "God save the King" and let the day staff take over.'

Bridie sang it with the rest of us though it must have worried her. She made no secret that she was what Mick-Joe called 'a red-hot republican'. Had she not taught me the Catholic history of the Republican movement?

The National Anthem came to an end, sung with rousing enthusiasm. Bridie stood by my side and sang like a lark. She walked in beauty these days and she smiled at me as she left my side.

'Remember, I sang your song, Miss Shanne.'

Out in the full dawning of the day, the last of the equipment was being moved in by the troops. There was no sign of the convoy. Mick-Joe appeared at my side and told me never to believe in Army time-tables.

'That convoy will appear when it's ready and not before. Give it a few days yet. Dublin is in a bitter action. They say the entire city's burning. We have no knowledge that tell us it's not. The people have come out from the slums and there's looting in the big shops like Clery's of Sackville Street. I had it from the major. The rebels are holding strong points. The Royal College of Surgeons in St Stephen's Green is defended and Boland's Mill and Jacob's Biscuit Factory. The looting is bad. They

110

smash the plate glass windows and they've took frieze coats and bolts of cloth against the winter ... loaves of fresh bread and boxes of chocolates ... cases of whiskey and wine ... hams and poultry and meat ... sides of beef and lamb. There was nothing that they haven't grabbed quick ... but the thing that was terrible was the bare feet, that, and the boots under the fur coats ... and the excitement in their eyes, as if they was off their heads entirely. It's a real war we have in Dublin this minute and dead men lying in the streets. The priests are doing overtime getting the poor souls to heaven.'

'Is it any good trying to ship the cattle from the station?' I asked him to change the subject, and he took off his cap and scratched his head.

'The train will go as usual.'

It was a job I hated, but Sister Sullivan had given me leave to take time off to load the frightened cattle for the docks at the North Wall. I had had two years to get used to it now and this morning was bad. Dermot was due out this morning. I had decided to cancel him ... and had forgotten. We had made a pet of him ... a fool thing to do. He would never run smoothly away from home. The clanking of the trucks was a terror. He made a bid for liberty and pushed his slavering muzzle into my hand. There was no hope of liberty and I knew the value of liberty by now. I told Mick-Joe to have him put off the truck and taken back to Merton, where he belonged.

The groom shook his head at me in sorrow, but in anger too.

'It was something to do with Master Dermot's birthday. The orange telegram, but it is all past and there's no sense in it,' he said. 'I'm glad you haven't to starve. There's a paradise in your head and not misery always at you. At the same time, that little bullock brung back our luck. I think it's right to take him home and leave him bide in the paddock, but the drovers will be thinking we're a right pair of "eegits". Shure ye all treated that little gentleman as if he was a pet kitten, the first weeks of his life.'

'We wanted something to love,' I murmured. 'We'll not sell him now. He kept the laughter living in our hearts, when it had all gone a long time.'

'You stood firm on your two feet, Miss, when the world died about us and the whole future was blazing before us, with what was coming. You didn't even see it ... and now you'll be happy with the little creature in the paddock and Selina with the peelings for him after dinner every night and yourself paying a visit to him every time you come near Merton.'

Monday, Tuesday, Wednesday, Thursday, Friday ... I was worrying about Selina, still not back from Dublin. She might have vanished off the face of the earth and I knew that civilians were being killed in the streets of the city.

'They even shell their own troops an odd time, the Army,' Mick-Joe said, and I laughed him to scorn and did not know which army he meant. 'That's how it is with armies, all the world over,' he said.

I told him that staff officers would never allow such a thing to happen. Staff officers saw everything was properly run.

'Is it the fellas with the red bands and the scramble egg on their caps? They're the worst of all, Miss. They can't even boil wather.'

There was no news of the convoy either, far less Selina. Then news came from Merton that she was safely home. Her mother was in hospital and recovering, but she would be kept in for safety. There had been the worst battle so far in Dublin, right near the flat where the old lady lived. They had been lucky to come alive out of it. Father sent for me to go to Merton at once. Selina would not be happy till she saw me. I was to bring the groom with me. It was not safe to travel alone these days. Mrs Geraghty would have the gates standing open for us...

Mick-Joe and I cantered side by side along the road to Merton and indeed there was Mrs Geraghty standing waiting for us. She was gracious enough to accompany us a hundred yards along the drive to tell us the news. Selina had come home safe from the bloodiest battle the land had ever known. She had looked terrible when she came first, but there was a very nice man had brung her the last bit of the way. Back in Merton, she busied herself about the breakfast and was just as careful about the doctor's fried rashers as she always was.

'There was nobody ever like Selina, nor ever will be,' I said.

I knew it was so and prayed for Jesus, Mary and Holy St Joseph to keep her deep in their loving care and then knew it for a very Roman Catholic prayer, but what harm?

We went down past the damson-tree corner and on round to the stables and Mick-Joe took the horses in charge, while I ran along the path to the kitchen.

I opened the door and searched the crowded familiar room and found her and the next moment she had me in her arms.

Everybody was there. I saw so many familiar people and strange ones too. Mick-Joe passed me in a moment and muttered to me that I was making a holy show of myself. Selina was the centre of attraction and there was a group round the big open hearth. I saw Sally and Bridie and Marcella. Mrs Geraghty had followed us in. The 'hen woman' was hiding in a dark corner. A stranger, who had brought Selina home from Drumcullan, was being nobly entertained to two bottles of stout.

I returned my attention to Selina and was foolish enough to say I had feared that I was never going to see her again and she surprised

114

me by bursting into bitter laughter.

'Do you know they ambushed the British, just landed from England?' she cried. 'The poor boys hadn't much idea if they weren't in Flanders. They were marching in along the Kingston Road and maybe wondering why people were giving them cigarettes or cups of tea. The rebels opened fire on them at Mount Street Bridge ... cut them to bits. It's no good thinking of it, for war is war, but it was a pity they has to set poor old Mam's flat ablaze. I grabbed her into my arms and ran with her up out into the street. It's no good to tell ye what it was like outside, for the gates of hell are not different.'

There had been a major battle ... Republican against regular Army troops ... this paradox of Ireland fighting the Irish ... born and bred.

They had been shelling the canal and hitting the houses. The old woman was wrapped warm in a shawl and Selina with her ran as fast as she could. The hospital reached to get her through its gates. They would be safe there.

'If ever I see an angel, I saw one then,' Selina said. 'She gave me a cup of tea and one to give the ma ... best tea we ever did have. The nurses bathed her and put her to bed and they were laughing at us and asking why we two ladies like ourselves so frit of a crashing of thunder? Yirrah! It was the queerest thunder I ever heard. I don't want to see anything like it

115

again. Every night I thank the doctors and nurses of Sir Patrick Dunne's Hospital, for they had the power on them to deliver a person from evil . . .'

Selina was a welcome patient, for she was not one to sit idle. 'They were wanting helping hands and I told them I was the cook at Merton. I can see the young nurse now and she telling me I had good references.

'It was quiet enough to get patients home after a bit . . . not the old mother, but others.'

The battle was fierce while it lasted and the flat was burnt, but there was no hurry for the old lady to leave the hospital for a week or two. It happened that they wanted to discharge an elderly man home after an operation and they had taken a fancy to Selina and she was anxious to get home to Merton. It was all arranged for her. If she accompanied a Mr Thaddeus O'Grady by cab to the train and then home to Drumcullen to the gentleman's house, it was easy enough for old Thaddeus to send Selina the ten miles to Merton with a fine trotting horse . . . And so it was done.

So Selina saw the spectacle of the centre of Dublin in revolution . . . saw Sackville Street, looted and afire and the big plate glass of the shops littering the street . . . saw the General Post Office under siege and maybe the flag still flying. She was glad to see green fields again. She was glad when the train got safe to Drumcullen and the Master of Drumcullan was safe tucked into his bed. The next morning, she made the easy drive to Merton with a very civil groom and the family all saw her off with grateful thanks. Now came the ru-rum-ra in the kitchen and the hot strong tea on the hob and the scones dripping butter. There was a great turf fire on the hearth, that maybe gave thanks to God for His mercy.

Maybe it was a feudal system at Merton, or the remnants of it, but they were all our people. Yet I know they should have complete freedom too. My thoughts were revolutionary to a certain extent. I knew myself an owl, that turned its head, round and round and round and round.

Selina saw us off at last and told me to mind every foot of the way.

'They're saying you're gone to the side of Britain and you truly Irish, Miss, born and bred, but you must help the King's soldiers ... to mend the broken ones, because of Mr Dermot, rest his soul!'

'Aren't we all Irish?' muttered Mick-Joe, 'and now brother will fight brother and Mary will weep tears in heaven, because of what's happening to her sons ...'

We rode slowly back to the home along the leafy road to the great stone steps.

'And this thing about the "prisoner of war status"?' I asked and again the groom shook his head sadly.

'The British will never grant it,' he said, 'and

the rebels know it. Pearse knew it and he'll be executed. All the ones that signed the Proclamation were prepared for the blood sacrifice.'

Father had told me the same thing an hour before and I thought of it again.

'It won't be an end to it, Honey. Britain always makes martyrs. There's nobody as immortal as a martyr. Remember that.'

He changed the subject then and sprung a surprise on me.

'Gareth Chandos is a very honourable young man, child. Last night, he asked my permission to pay court to you. He'd be right for you too. He's French extraction and goes back to the Wild Geese and Limerick and Sarsfield. Now he wants to wed my daughter. Why didn't you warn me? I thought you were still playing with dolls.'

I had known embarrassment and a scarlet face and he had been very amused. I asked him if he had given permission and he nodded his head and said it was up to me.

'I told you he was an honourable young man, didn't I?'

The honourable young man was waiting for me at the bottom of the steps and he may have wondered why I got so red in the face, but he sent the groom off with his horses and told me he had a special task for me. His next words put every other thought out of my head.

'The convoy will be at the gate very shortly,

118

Shanne. Turn back right away to the gate lodge and escort the outriders in. Let them have a welcome along the avenue.'

Mick-Joe suggested I might like to take his mount, muttered that Lady Gay couldn't abide outriders' motorcycles, but Gareth had some joke with himself and I had no choice but to go.

'So you want a rodeo show?' I said, and I thought he had Father's permission 'to pay court to me' and I was very happy indeed. I gritted my teeth as I met the first motorbikes coming through the big open gates. I could see that Gareth was watching me making an exhibition, but for once, Lady Gay behaved like an angel. I turned in the saddle and made a small bow to him, tipped the peak of my cap. Lady Gay was going to behave impeccably and my heart rejoiced. I pondered on giving an exhibition of haute ecole, as far as the steps and then discarded the idea as showing off.

The convoy had followed the outriders, ambulance after ambulance and one car after another. They were a goodly company and I thought they were far more than we expected. We seemed to have so few beds waiting for them. The nurses had come down to the steps to show a welcome and Gareth was strolling to take Lady Gay's rein.

'They've made a miscalculation,' he told me. 'They've sent us half times the count again, but they've filled in the ancillaries as well. They have nurses and all kinds of useful souls …

they've packed a quart into a pint pot, but not to worry. We'll move the beds over and make room. There's no sign of the matron yet, so Sister Sullivan will still act locum ...'

We settled in with no trouble in the world. The morale was high and everybody had come home. It was like the feeding of the five thousand. We pushed beds closer together. It was like a little miracle. You just stretched out a hand for something and it was there. My world was rose-pink just because Gareth had asked my father 'for my hand'. The day flew by on wings and everything was happy. Strangers smiled and accepted us as friends. Nothing was too much trouble. We got to work on the galleries, where there was so much spare space. We moved the beds and the galleries seemed to grow enormous.

I avoided Gareth on purpose, for I was shy of him. Then I missed the Phillips, Caroline and her husband, parents of Dermot and Rory. Even Blackie was not to be seen. I ran them to earth and found they had taken refuge in the library, which was their private territory. I had wondered if this might happen ... and it had. Aunt Caroline was in the old man's arms and her eyes red with weeping. 'The boys' had not come home. It had been an impossible dream, that Dermot and Rory would come too. God knew, I had had it myself and knew it was impossible. There was a time I had prayed for miracles. There should be something I could say, but my mouth was dumb. What was there to say? Nothing. I sat on the window ledge and knew the blank in my heart, that would never heal, and I knew the finality of death. I caught my knee in my hands and listened to my voice and I did not know what I said. It just came to me as I spoke.

'I think they did come ... both of them ... not in the flesh but in the brightness of spirit they had ... in the eternity they inherited. There was a time today, I felt that they possessed the whole house and will possess it for ever ...

'Look at Blackie,' I said. 'He knows it too.'

Perhaps Blackie was in transports because of the sound of my beloved voice, but I know that dogs sense things that we know nothing of.

'You made a memorial for them. It was a wonderful thing you did. It's like the memorial that will be made for the rebels, who are dying for Ireland. You can't really kill people who die for their country ... "pro patria mori". I know it's true ... or feel it is. I'm only a girl and I have no sense at all, but today, I saw a miracle happen. The whole house turned in its sleep and lived again. Dermot and Rory are coming to stay, as long as the house stands ... I promise you ... unseen, just getting used to eternity ... and it's for a long time ...'

I was on nights on Ward six that week and I bent over a young man with fair hair. He was restless and wandering and had groaned in

121

his sleep.

'I can feel the pain still, worse than ever. How can I bear it when the leg's cut off? I know it's not cut off. I can feel it like a glowing coal, but it's gone true enough. I'll never feel the leaves under my feet, when it's Autumn again ... not Dingle Bay again ... nevermore, nevermore, nevermore ... like the bloody raven...'

Sister Sullivan was as skilled in the arts of war as Limerick City had been. She had brought small sugar-coated pills in a spoon ... warm milk for him to drink ... a hand on his brow.

'Go to sleep and rest easy,' she said. 'It's all quiet tonight and tomorrow will be another day.

'You must get used to these cases, Paul Revere,' she smiled at me. 'These lads will be a part of your life. There'll be many more of them. Put your head on the pillow and sleep beside him. Give him your company and a bit of your courage...'

'Johnnie my son, war isn't fun.
For when once it's begun it's a terrible
    thing.
Famine and woe for the high and the low
And a great deal more than drumming,
    you know?'

Her Irish brogue was soft and gentle, as she whispered to me to steal a little sleep. I would have to be off early in the morning to see to the farm at Merton and the rest would do me no harm.

I went to Merton by the side track past the paddock, so that I could visit the calf. It was strange the way we thought of him still as a calf and I daresay we always would though he was well-grown now. He was watching through the gate for me. I brought a hay-bag of sweet sanfoin and a pocketful of calf nuts and he danced a song for me with the delight on his heart. Tonight, I knew he would watch for Sally or maybe Selina herself to come along to say goodnight to him with a colander filled with the peelings and the scraps.

Dermot...

It came into my brain from the past out of nowhere ... the thought of the orange telegram.

Regret to inform you ... Second Lieut Dermot Phillips ... Second Lieut Rory Phillips ... killed in action...

The orange telegram had laid a whole mansion in ruins. I had thought the calf was a talisman against evil. He was happy now as he kicked his heels against the sun. I felt a stab of guilt that I had felt such pleasure that Gareth had asked my father for permission to 'pay court to me'.

Maybe I was going to find happiness after all, after never hoping for it. The days were flying quickly past and there seemed no time for sadness. There were soldiers everywhere and nurses in plenty and youth. All day long, the political discussions echoed round the corridors and galleries ... pollen down the wind.

The rebellion was smouldering all through the Provinces,

'Pearse, the Dreamer will be crucified for his dreams.'

'They knew the price they had to pay.'

'But we're all Irish too and we're fighting for Britain and our fathers joined up for Britain in Africa against the Boers.'

All day long, the arguments went on, till somebody yelled at them to shut up and have some peace.

'The rebels were "the lower orders". They had started trouble in the most important war of all time, but they had been kept under. You could not deny that. They hadn't a chance.'

There was a loud clear voice from the top gallery ... Oxford or Cambridge giving tongue.

'They ran their jobs in bare feet, but I'll tell you one thing. If they shoot the signatories now and don't give PoW status, they'll never hold rebel Ireland. It will be Freedom when the time is right ... and good luck to them.'

'And there's Cambridge University Debating Society for you,' declared a rich Irish brogue. 'If we all sat down and thought about it, we're on the same side. We'd be better to stick to Landsdowne Rd. At least we'd have a kick at the ball.'

One day, Gareth took me to sit in one of the window engravures, after rounds. We overlooked the whole gardens and watched Blackie, who was taking patients for a walk. As usual he had a ball in his mouth and put it down at intervals in strategic positions at his guests' feet.

'Why can I never make up my mind about Ireland, Gareth? Always I see things in two lights. There are so many opinions...'

'I think it is quite usual to have the two-way view,' he said. 'I expect that Bridie filled you in on the Siege of Limerick. I know we've discussed it before.'

I nodded my head and remembered Mick-Joe talking to me, I think it was after Mother's funeral and he had kidnapped me and we were in a hazel-nut grove on the side of a furzy hill and the blackberries past for that year. Mick-Joe had been trying to warn me of the trouble that was coming. The day came back to me now, very vividly. I remembered the date, when Ireland had had the last great defeat of all the defeats, and Sarsfield had marched out of Limerick to exile in France in the service of one of the Louis, with the 'Wild Geese'.

I blew my breath on the window pane and wrote with my finger.

1691

'That's right,' said Gareth and wrote diagonally across it.

125

'Same conflict,' he murmured and then he went on:

'Richard Chandos was my ancestor and he was in the Irish Army. As far as we know he was an expert in the art of the sabre and the epée, and he was in the Siege of Limerick and went into exile. He may have been French to start with for there is an idea he might have been mixed up with the Huguenots. It's vague, but there's no doubt that he flew with the "Wild Geese" and was a soldier under Sarsfield till his death ... Sarsfield on the field at Landen...'

I asked him to tell me more of it and it struck me that he was very uneasy. Maybe he was working up to a proposal of marriage? That made me blush and I was shy with him.

'The Irish armies were mostly Catholic. It was strange that he was a Protestant or anyway not Catholic ... the Chandos descendants have always been Protestant. It would be all right.'

Maybe he had shown his intentions too soon. Suddenly he was confused and said he must stop boring me with history again. I had had enough of it from Bridie with the washing on Friday nights. He laughed too much at that and tried to change the subject, but I pinned him to it, asked him what happened next.

'Richard married a lady ... an Irish lady of great beauty and high rank. She owned a vineyard and it became Chandos et Fils, and it's still that now, hundreds of years on. That Irish lady is in a portrait on the main staircase of the chateau. The first time I saw you, I thought you had a look of her.'

So the family lived in a chateau, I thought, and now I knew that he was going to attempt 'to pay court to me'. I felt like a frightened fawn and said I must not stay off the ward much longer, but he took my hand in his and said I was working too hard. Would I not like to walk with him in the spinney for a little while? There was nothing else I could do for he held my hand tightly and we reached the spinney in record time. We came on a soldier and a nurse kissing under the first tree, so we turned home by the river. Arrived there, we looked into the pool to see if the trout was in sight and he was not. In a sort of desperation, Gareth took my shoulders between his hands and I felt the shock, that electrified me. I knew he was the one for me, but I was shy as he was and he lost his nerve, having told me he wanted to talk to me.

He changed back to politics.

'Write this "Prisoner of War" thing out of your head. There's no hope of it. You'll not run into trouble with the rebels, for Red Cross puts you in the clear, but don't talk about any sort of politics. If you must do it, come to me and to nobody else...'

If this was love, I was moving in a rose-pink world. I thought that maybe Dermot was a fading ghost that had moved into the past and knew myself guilty, but Caroline Phillips spoke to me one day and told me that it was obvious that Gareth was in love with me.

'When he asks you, my dear, say yes to him. Toby and I don't want you to turn into a Miss Havisham. We want your children for Screebogue one day ... as if they were our boy's children. Dermot will be happy too ... and the little red bull will be a token, that it will come right...'

She took herself off quickly and she said nothing more. Chandos continued to seek me out and I talked politics with him, as if I was learning the art of the epée, like his ancestor taught it. I asked him to try to get me a copy of the Proclamation again and my mind skidded about the words of it.

'Irish men and Irish women, in the name of God and of the dead generations, from whom she receives her old tradition of nationhood, Ireland through us, summons her children to her flag and strikes for her freedom...'

My mind dreamed for a moment and ran on '... supported by her children in America and by gallant allies in Europe...'

And that would be the emigrants from the famine ... the Great Hunger and maybe the

128

Wild Geese many years on.

Then the proclamation again...

'She strikes in full confidence of victory ... We declare the right of the people to the ownership of Ireland and to the unfettered control of Irish destiny...

'The long suppression of that right by a foreign people and government has not extinguished the right ... nor will it ever be extinguished, except by the destruction of the Irish people...'

Gareth sheep-dogged me. If he found me huddled in a corner with Bridie with our heads close together, he knew I was hearing the news from Dublin and told us to go and do the worst job he could think of, in the sluice rooms.

He looked at me now and told me to read the name of the signatories one more time. I was brooding too much on the Proclamation and I was not going to be allowed to borrow it any more.

He read them out loud for me.

'Thomas Clarke, Sean McDiarmaid, Thomas McDonough, P. H. Pearse, Ceeannt, Connolly, Plunkett.'

The French intonation was noticeable, when he was put out with me.

'They signed their death warrants. Now the convict ships will fill the British jails. There are few dreams in jails and hunger strikes are an abomination to God!'

He gave a great sigh.

129

'Pearse said that Dublin would be a shining city. If they did not win the war, they deserved to win it. Pearse said they would win it in death. I think he spoke the truth.'

'Please Gareth. Now you are leading me into talking politics but tell me who I am. Have I the birthright of this side of the Pale? Why should I be clothed and well fed? I am as Irish as any of the poor. I am as Irish as the Irish themselves. Why should Bridie's widowed mother have had to do our washing? Why should her children have had to run with no shoes in winter?'

I turned to Gareth with appeal in my eyes.

'I want no part of war. Always my people have made war for Britain. Otherwise how could I wear the Red Cross uniform? Why should I have been shot at that day for summoning the nurses? The Red Cross is neutral. Then again, I had to take to farming because we were broke. As soon as I did that, I was snubbed by the so-called gentry ... the Protestant ascendancy, but it was no matter to me. I want no part of war. I just want to mend broken soldiers, as somebody said. In a kind of way by doing that, I've made war for the Allies. Then we had to make Merton support itself or they would all have been out of work. They understood and they were willing to help and able to do it. We were a kind of a family really and we were friends. They have been wonderful people ... wept for my griefs, truly

130

cared. They were far more valuable than any crock of gold I might have found.'

I found myself opening my heart to Gareth. I knew I should have held my tongue, but I could not.

It all came out about the nights I had seen men on the run ... seen them in the darkness of the night and stitched up bullet wounds, not stitched them up but bound them.

He took me into his arms and held me close to him, told me he had known about this.

'It was the right thing to do, my little rabbit. You were in an impossible position, aged maybe fourteen, fifteen, and with big trouble all about you. You just refused to close the dispensary door to what you knew were hurt birds, and you were a country girl. You knew that a wild bird died, if you shut it in a cage.'

I wept in his arms and was comforted and went back to the forbidden politics again.

'They weren't bad men, or I thought they weren't. Pearse was promising freedom, just as Abraham Lincoln did...'

'And you promise to give up discussing all these state affairs and getting involved with rebellions.'

He took my face between his hands and kissed me first on one cheek and then another. Then he looked at me silently for a long minute and last of all, he laid his mouth very gently over mine.

'I love you very much, Paul Revere,' he said

against my lips. Then he took my hand and walked with me, till we came to a solitary garden seat and there Blackie found us and he had come equipped with a tennis ball, so we had some business to do to ease our shyness, for it was a new world for both of us, or I thought so.

'I'll not take sides any more,' I said in a low voice. 'I'll mend broken soldiers, but still I'll not close my eyes to hurt birds. I don't agree with wars or rebellions, nor in murders, nor hangings, nor yet in falseness nor in meanness, or in cruelty and neglect. I just believe in happiness. I give you my word on it.'

He took the tennis ball and flung it into the middle of the shrubbery and it was to give Blackie a nice long search, but Blackie was as enthusiastic as ever. I remembered a forgotten world, where Dermot and Rory and I used to throw the ball into the lake to slow the dog up and how he would plunge in and come back and shake himself all over us and then look up for more play. If we tired him at cricket he was quite clever enough to take the ball into the middle of the gold-fish pool and sit with it in his mouth, while he cooled off. The fish had no fear of him, they circulated quite happily about his black back.

I knew that I was still Miss Facing-Both-Ways. There was no working myself out in any sense, but I was Irish, right or wrong and nobody could steal my birthright from me.

132

'Go on mending broken soldiers, Shanne. You're very good at it. You mended me with gentleness and great skill. My life has a new brightness about it, for the ward swings open and you come in and so many people have excuses to seek you out. I find I have maybe to wait in a British queue, if I want a dressing tray for a patient.'

He threw the ball right across the croquet lawn and as far as the tennis courts and Blackie was away like a shot.

'The garden is standing a tip-toe to welcome Shanne. The gorse on the hills has never been so bright, because l'amour is in love.'

He took me close in his arms as if he never meant to let me go and I knew I would have stayed in his arms for the rest of my life.

There was a bell ringing three times and that meant an emergency. We were both on duty for emergencies and with three rings, there was no time for delay. We walked quickly to the hall and Blackie came galloping after us to see what was wrong. By the droop of his tail and the look in his eyes, I could see he felt just as disappointed as I was.

'Go on mending broken soldiers, Shanne. You're very good at it. You mended me with gentleness and great skill. My life has a new brightness about it, for the ward swings open and you come in and so many people have excuses to seek you out. I find I have maybe to wait in a British queue, if I want a dressing tray for a patient.'

He threw the ball right across the croquet lawn and as far as the tennis courts and Blackie was away like a shot.

'The garden is standing a tip-toe to welcome Shanne. The gorse on the hills has never been so bright, because l'amour is in love.'

He took me close in his arms as if he never meant to let me go and I knew I would have stayed in his arms for the rest of my life.

There was a bell ringing three times and that meant an emergency. We were both on duty for emergencies and with three rings, there was no time for delay. We walked quickly to the hall and Blackie came galloping after us to see what was wrong. By the droop of his tail and the look in his eyes, I could see he felt just as disappointed as I was.

PART THREE

THE MATRON

From life to death might be the snap of a finger. How often it was to be like that and there was a red alert up in the front hall. We were wanted in the ward, that I had got accustomed to thinking of as 'mine', though it was no such thing. Father was there and Sister Geraldine and Joanne and one or two of the VADs but there seemed to me no great panic. One of the patients had noticed his wound was bleeding and he had called the Sister and she had sent for help. She knew well that it was bad ... a secondary haemorrhage from an artery and days after the operation.

Sister Geraldine had alerted the theatre and it was ready by the time Gareth and I arrived. Father invited me to come and count swabs, said he himself would be giving the anaesthetic. Luckily the chap had an empty stomach. It was a pity I had not been present. I was a great expert on tourniquets, but they had had to go on without me and that, of course, was a joke that never wore out with him.

It all moved along efficiently, but it was complicated. I thought there was a great deal of blood and indeed there was. I know I got a great deal on myself, but so did everybody else. I was glad I was not alone in the big dispensary at Merton, for I remembered the fear and the longing for Father to come home from his rounds...

I thought that we had all started whiter than white and now I knew myself as an abattoir attendant...but the bleeding had stopped and soon the patient was in bed in the ante-room.

Bridie supplied us with coffee and the team, as they called themselves, were reliving the battle. I excused myself and made for the ablutions and Bridie was kind enough to follow me up and make a pile of most of my clothes, before she doused me with water. I had even got blood in my hair, so she shoved my head in a basin of cold water and got me fairly spotless. Then she wound a hand towel round my head for a turban and followed that up by borrowing a terry-towelling bath-robe off a peg and wrapping it round me. It was far too big for me and it had HOTEL SCRIBE, PARIS embroidered across the back in red.

She told me to give it back to her when I had changed and she would see to getting it washed and returned.

'It belongs to Mr Gareth. He won't mind you using it.'

She disappeared, before I could say any more and I heard the others coming along the corridor. I went at a run in bare feet, straight in the direction of the bed-rooms, tripped a few times, till I grabbed the hem into both hands. I was halted by the view across the hall and down to the steps. An important lady

138

personage was arriving. A staff car had disgorged itself at the bottom of the front steps and up the steps had come this lady, very sure of herself, flanked by a senior officer. 'His uniform had never seen the field'. I could hear Mick-Joe's voice again. This was what he called 'a Brass Hat', who was not capable of boiling water. The lady had reached the hall and she paused to push back her motoring veil, to reveal a lovely sable hat with a rose arranged under the brim of it ... perfection.

'You have nobody standing by to welcome you, Madam,' said Brass Hat and I realised the predicament I found myself in. There was no escape. I could only give myself up. It was obvious what had happened. There had been a rumour drifting in Screebogue House that Matron was on her way at last and that we must watch out, because 'she was a tartar'. Mick-Joe refused to 'turn the Major out of Matron's office, till it was definite'. He had packed the files ready to go and put in a fresh blotter. He had even put a new typing ribbon in her machine. Next door he had fixed a new office for the Major, but till Matron had arrived 'he refused to disturb Gareth'. It would only take ten minutes flat, he had assured us, to do the transformation scene...

I wondered why he had disappeared, just when we wanted him, and saw him appear like a magic genie. I had an ally, well tried and trusted. I could see him working inside the glass door, but he was out of sight of the Matron, who had cut me off from the stairs, so that I was captive. I grabbed the hem of the robe between my fists and prepared for a run, but there was no chance of it.

'You surely had my signals?' she demanded of me and I knew it might be best to play for time. The Matron's door opened and the little IN/OUT notice was changed quietly. It seemed that Mrs Love was in. Along the hall, Major Gareth Chandos was out. I could imagine the changing of the files and the fresh blotter and flowers that I had left on Gareth's desk being grabbed and put fresh out for Matron. I shook my head and Brass Hat glared at me.

'There was an emergency in the theatre,' I mumbled.

'It seemed to disorganise the whole house,' he remarked and I denied that such a thing was possible.

'You'd better see to serving breakfast at once in my office,' Mrs Love said. 'Get yourself changed and in correct kit. You've not even told me your name and rank, but you're pretty "sans culotte" and you have not even identified yourself.'

'I'm Shanne,' I muttered like 'a half-eejit' and Mrs Love sneered at that and asked me if I was a gun-dog and I said I was not, added that we had a very fine gun-dog called Blackie and she must meet him presently...

I was very pleased to see Mick-Joe come out

140

of the door of what was not Gareth's office any longer and advance across the hall to us. He gave a magnificent salute to the new arrivals and told Mrs Love that her breakfast would be served in ten minutes, if she went through the door in front of her.

'A hundred thousand welcomes, Matron,' he said. 'Our eyes are weary with watching the road for you to come.'

'I can't make head or tail of you,' Mrs Love said to me. 'Report to me this evening, when I've had time to settle in. Your showing this morning is a disgrace. I won't tolerate slovens. Now let's see if the kitchens can do better. I must have discipline. I'll not tolerate streals. Don't ever think it for one minute. Now take yourself off at once out of my sight.'

I scurried up the stairs like a demented rabbit and tripped a few times on the way over the hem of the dressing gown, landed on the bed at last and lay there shaking with a strange fear that possessed me. I had a premonition that this woman was like 'the Horla' that had come into the house. God knows what would happen before her evil spirit departed from here.

At that moment I even thought she might have to be exorcised, but I was full of strange fancies, for I was very tired. As it was, nothing happened. I made no appointment to see her and she made no attempt to get to know me. She never recognised me, as Father's daughter, and she ignored me completely and I was glad of it. She was disliked by one and all for she was a martinet. I held my tongue and avoided her.

I had seen her as a very beautiful woman, 'a boss woman' sharp as a vixen. I should have made sure that she was made welcome and asked her to Merton House for dinner, but I had no welcome for her, and the fault was mine from the beginning. I could think of nothing but Mother's grave, and the honeysuckle that had fallen on the coffin.

Louise Gregg. 1878–1914. My heart was like flint.

I did not think it would ever change, not in the years that followed, but perhaps it did.

Within a day or two, I saw the way she looked at Father, and made much of him.

If I close my eyes now, I can see her as clearly as if it was that first day of all, when she appeared at the head of the main table in the Refectory. It was her first public appearance at supper time and she was wearing a dark blue well-cut uniform. She had medal ribbons on her breast and a gold fob-watch. Her collar was stiff, white, starched, high in the neck like an Eton schoolboy's. She wore a flowing bow, such as an artist might wear. Her cap was typical of one of the big London hospitals ... dark naval material for the dress, but square like a box for the cap and white ... She was a character out of *Alice in Wonderland*. 'Off with her head!' The cap had lit on her head and perched high. It never seemed lost to its elegance and its positioning.

We all sat waiting for her to make her entrance and SHE came as the clock struck seven and looked all round the room. The tables were arranged geometrically and the men able to walk were allocated to their places, according to rank and name. The nurses were at their own tables, but one was put at the head of each of the soldiers' tables, to see to their diets and maybe their behaviour.

She looked slowly round and missed nothing with her critical eye.

'Please stand,' she said. 'We'll get to know each other over the coming weeks. I hope we will have a happy ship here. Thank you.'

We had planned such a pleasant home at Screebogue and it seemed that we had succeeded, though we were crowded to capacity. The standards of discipline shot high with the advent of Isobel Love. I do not think that happiness increased, for discipline was now iron hard. There was nothing one could put a finger on. She had ignored the loss of welcome at the time of her arrival. I never asked for an appointment to see her. She ignored me. Like a fool, I ignored her arrival or any mention of it. If I had sense, I might have winkled them out of the theatre ... Father, Sister Fitz, Gareth. It would have made a marvellous joke. I ignored any mention of it. She did not even know who this strange girl

143

was, dressed in the Scribe Hotel dressing gown and the towelling turban.

God above! I showed her no politeness, just ignored the whole thing and avoided her. I should have acted with decent manners, but that first afternoon I was off duty and I acted with propriety. I cut lunch and sulked in the paddock with Dermot, the calf: I appeared at supper, very correctly clad and by that time, Brass Hat and his escorts had disappeared. Nobody had mentioned me by name and nobody had told *her* I was Father's daughter.

Thereafter, she and I avoided each other. It was my duty to invite her to Merton House for supper. Father and Gareth had met her. The stubborn thought stuck in my heart. Louise Gregg was Father's wife and my mother. Isobel Love meant nothing to me. The days slid by and still Matron and I were strangers. Mick-Joe told me I was a fool, but I had a kind of apathy. Then one evening, when I was on duty, Father drove her home in the gig and she stayed to supper at Merton House. Another time, he came to the evening meal at the home and she had a special dinner sent into her office there, waited on by Bridie. 'Nobody has even told her who Miss Shanne is,' Bridie had muttered to Mick-Joe and he sought me out ... a kind of delegation.

'Are you gone blind?' he demanded. 'She knows he's a widower but nobody has seen fit to acquaint her who "Shanne" is and ye don't see what's happening. Do you not know how she has the knack of keeping whiskey locked in her filing cabinet. Do you know how she has the art of plying him with it? No fool is worse than an old fool, but you have the behaviour of a young fool and no sense at all, at all. She has changed you to night duty with Sister Sullivan and she often comes to sup at the home. I drive him home to Merton House and often as not, I have to help him to bed. There are evenings when she comes to Merton House to dine and they all know it. I have to drive her back to Screebogue afterwards and "thank you, Michael", she says and sweeps off up the steps like a duchess.'

He looked at me and sighed. 'Perhaps, she got you out of the way by putting you on nights, but it's my opinion that she just doesn't know who you are, for if she did, she'd be working at it. That one is after a rich husband and maybe she doesn't know the true facts of the case. I've been sent by the others from Merton to put a word in your ear.'

Yet Matron and I circled each other like Kilkenny cats and no word between us. I was in error. I know it now. I left the door open and the horse escaped. I opened my eyes at last and knew it was too late. She was paying too much attention to the CO, my father. To her I was just one of the nurses, who had dressed herself up in a Hotel Scribe dressing robe and wound a turban round her head, a girl, who had a name

145

like a gun-dog's...

It was quite impossible for such a thing to have happened and I knew it was my own fault.

Time went on and still the situation was not changed. I could not go to her now and say 'I'm the CO's daughter'. It was all too late. The occasion never arose. It went on as before.

I worked at the farm as usual, swapping afternoons for nights. I rarely saw her, hardly spoke to her. I knew that Father was besotted with her. Even at Merton, they seemed strangers to me. One day, I must invite her to Merton House, but not yet. Maybe my heart lay in the grave with Louise Gregg. I busied myself with the affairs of the Home. It was a wonderful place and we had fifty patients now, all young men in their prime, given to falling in love with their nurses. It was our duty to keep them well cared for. We played croquet and tennis with them or accompanied them on walks with Blackie, through the silver birch copse that led down to the trout stream. It was a very happy existence and they were all getting better and the battlefield was calling some of them again.

The Great War was going badly. Tens of thousands of Irish-born men from the North and South of Ireland were fighting as Volunteers in the British Army. The Republicans had been cruelly punished. A great number had been executed, a great many sent to prison in Ireland and Wales and

England. The rest of the rebels carried on the rebellion, as best they could. Many of them took to the hills, that place of the curlews, or they worked like moles in their prisons, plotting the future ... and martyrs had been made a-plenty. If the prisoners had been given 'prisoner of war status', it might have been different, but change was in the air. Freedom would come one day, but not yet. The electoral register was changing. Women might be given the vote and who had ever heard such a thing? In 1919, De Valera, out of prison, was to go to America to ask for help, but that was all in the future. Ireland was still a distressful country and there was military action over all. Houses were raided for arms. Houses were burnt to the ground. There were trenches dug across roads and men were shot down at their own front doors by rebels and soldiers. I blotted out the thought of politics, for Gareth would have none of it and Gareth had attained a great importance in my mind. My thoughts narrowed down to the Screebogue Convalescent Home and the overseeing of Merton Farm and the fact that we were showing a profit at Merton House ... at last. So I closed my eyes to a great many things, even to the making of martyrs by the British Army. The lamenting for them had only started, but it had swung a whole nation after it.

There had been this shooting of 'prisoners of war'. The British powers that be had overlooked the fact that they were all Irish. One time, they had fought for Britain in every war there was. Look at Screebogue House now and most of them only senior school boys in the sixth form ... like Dermot and Rory Phillips ... In Screebogue, we had English soldiers, Irish born and Irish bred, from public schools and colleges ... Congowes Wood, Mountjoy, Portora, Downside, Trinity, Oxford, Cambridge...

I still tried to stay neutral and face-both-ways, but it was hard.

They were wounded and quite a proportion crippled. Mostly they worried that they would never get well enough to fight again. Morale was high. They had come to terms with their incapacity. We had this great mansion, packed with young warriors and they were the salt of God's earth ... and then it rained, for seven days. We were in short supply on crutches and wheel-chairs. It was a punishment to lie in bed, like a child. It rained and it rained and morale went down and the skies were grey. It was just that week, that was to be known as the 'the wet week'. It would not leave off raining and we were house-bound and snakes and ladders ran out and chess too.

So they had to come to terms with crippledom. It was going to be a very different life for some of them ... and it rained for ever and I was on the wards. Then the miracle happened. The 'Ortho van' arrived with supplies . . . crutches and wheel-chairs, walking frames and walking sticks . . . and months had gone by since Matron's arrival.

I looked out and saw the clock golf green was all small lakes. Blackie was in a terrible depression with his tennis ball in his mouth. I had them send up all the new equipment and then Mick-Joe told me that my father had hired a car and had taken Matron to the city for the day. Sister Sullivan had gone too 'to make it decent'.

Joanne Webb and I thought up 'the Polo-Pony' game. We proposed a plan and it was adopted. We would clear the second gallery of furniture and play 'Polo-Pony'. I looked out through one of the high windows and saw that the rain would never stop, so I told them in the hall to send up the new orthopaedic supplies to the ward in the long gallery. I told the patients what I intended to do and I collected a great many willing helpers. It was Sister Sullivan's day off. I was in charge. God help me!

It took us no time at all to move the beds back. What size was a polo field? We did not know, but it did not seem to matter. Blackie had a ball at once, a soft ball. We had a few wheel-chairs now and we had crutches for many. We had walking frames, that had taken ages to come. Joanne and I did not count teams. Maybe it was like the game at Eton? They all played in either direction. The whole company burst out singing like the birds, or so

149

it seemed. I will say that Joanne and I took care that they would not get hurt. We had appointed 'keepers and minders' and the score mattered nothing. It will always be denied, but I maintain that no game has ever been so enjoyed since. It was if we dropped a lighted match into a straw stack. There was a transport of spirits from low to high. Looking back, I know Matron was right and I was in the wrong, but it was a pity their car broke down and they had to turn home.

We had collected most of the patients to the top gallery, nurses and all. They ringed the whole place and there were no rules to the game, only that everybody should be happy. The noise was appalling, but no complaints were heard. There were so many nurses spread about that everybody was in good care. We were all very 'high'. I admit that.

Anybody keen on playing was provided with a croquet mallet or a walking stick. The top gallery was crowded with players, when it had been swept clear of beds. An audience collected from all over ... kitchens, halls, stairs. Blackie came up and set a tennis ball at my feet and somebody blew a whistle. The game was on. The laughter was like a rookery of crows on a May morning. There was nobody to disapprove. My father was on his way to the city in a hired car and Matron was with him. They had taken Sister Sullivan with them as a chaperone. I was trying to keep order and

150

making a poor job of it. Nobody wanted order, as Joanne pointed out. Still we both played for safety. The men in the wheel-chairs had two helpers. The men on crutches had two sides to grab them if they fell. Nobody seemed to mind what direction the teams played. It was like the Eton Wall game, somebody explained and that was clear enough. It was an enchanted game, straight out of the pages of *Alice in Wonderland.*

'These wheel-chairs steer like tanks. I don't know how old ladies ever manage them,' panted Captain McLean as he went past me at three miles an hour, with two kilted Highlanders in close attendance.

We were having a wonderful time. It was a great pity that Father was no good with cars. It was a great pity that he had not taken a driver. Ten miles along the Dublin road, the car died and it took a long time to resuscitate it … a very long time indeed. It was hours before they turned home, and then they were all in fighting humour, as it happens on such days.

Father and his company must have arrived home well after lunch time and the 'Polo-Pony' was well into the second half and hysterical. Maybe it was all very bad for the patients, but this I will never admit. We had had a wonderful time and the gallery was crowded to capacity. Lunch had been postponed and even the kitchen staff were present, cheering their favourites on to victory. There was plenty of time for lunch afterwards, but it was time to blow the whistle anyway. I put it to my lips and thought, enough was enough. At the same time, there was a sudden silence ... as if an angel had passed overhead. I noticed the hush and faces that grew apprehensive. I noticed the people who looked sideways and crept out of the way. The whole scene came to a halt and people were fixed 'in aspic', as if they were playing 'Statues'. A great sigh went up into the silence. I had not heard the car arrive or the voices in the hall. Blackie's tail was between his legs and he was crouched down by my side. The patients were quitting the 'field'. Only Joanne stood by my side at the head of the gallery. Up the stairs very regally came the Matron. She was looking splendid in her dark dress uniform. She seemed to have gained stature in my eyes. Almost I heard her cry 'Off with her head'.

The company mostly forsook us and fled. I do not think either Joanne or I could have spoken, or moved, to save our lives. When I did speak, it was with the voice of a stranger.

'Some Orthopaedic stuff came this morning, Madame, after you left. It's been dreary with all the rain. We decided to clear the gallery and play "Polo-Pony" with a soft ball and some of the crutches and the odd wheel-chair and that. It has been a great success.'

'Has it?' she said. 'Has it indeed?'

I could see the staff doing their best to get the

gallery beds in place and the patients back to 'the status quo', all as silent as mice. I wondered where Father was and wished he would come to my rescue, for I knew I would have no mercy from Isobel Love.

Gareth had gone somewhere for the day...

She was a formidable figure with the dark navy uniform and the high white collar and the strange highly-perched hat.

Her skirt whisked the stairs, as she came up and I thought she was an angry cat, that lashed her tail in fury.

The staff who had run at the sight of her came creeping back.

'I gave no authority to use the new equipment,' she said and I admitted that the fault was mine. Joanne said that she must claim some of the credit and added that it had all gone like a bomb and the sun had shone again, after a week of rain. Loyal Joanne!

'You are both a disgrace to your unit,' she said. 'There will be investigation in depth and heads will fall for this.'

She looked into my eyes and hated me and at last she recognised the girl, that first day in the 'Hotel Scribe' dressing gown. I could see her turning it all in her head and wondering who I was. The men had come over and were pleading our case ... said they had begged to try the equipment and no harm had been done. 'It was the best game of "Polo-Pony" and we all laughed ourselves silly and nobody won.'

153

'I want you to come to my study, Miss Shanne,' she said. 'You have no business to take over new orthopaedic equipment ... It may be necessary to get you out of Screebogue House, back to that farm you think so much of.' She glared at me.

'You're not entitled to touch "Orthopaedics". You're not even SRN. You're just a Red Cross nurse, and that's nothing.'

I looked at her in despair and started to plead.

'I go down to Merton House at seven most mornings to see to the milking. I have permission to do it. I have leave to attend Ballymahon every market day and I go to Carrickboy with the Merton House butter and eggs. We were short of money, after my mother died. We all helped and the farm's a success now. Father said nobody would object. We're got into credit now, and Mick-Joe managed the most of it. I could not have done it without him or Sally or Selina ... even Bridie an odd while.'

I could almost see the clock wheels spinning in her brain as she tried to understand what I was babbling about. I could see a strange dawn of realisation, as to who I might be. I had a great rush of relief when Father came slowly up the stairs and took in the whole situation. He was in uniform today, which was not unusual under Matron's influence. I was glad to see the

Sam Brown and the military spit and polish; that was 'Mick-Joe'.

'Has my girl being breaking all the rules, Isobel? Don't be too hard on her. She's had the hell of a time, since Louise died. It was Miss Byrnes made her come here. She was to marry Dermot Phillips, who was lost with his brother in Flanders. It was the end of the Screebogue dynasty, but she's helped the family to survive, maybe the old gun-dog too. Poor Shanne ... never called anything else, but "Shanne".'

Isobel Love saw her mistake. I could still see the cogs of her brain ticking over. Somehow maybe she had missed the queen of hearts for nothing but the girl in the 'Hotel Scribe' dressing gown ... had thought of her as a girl of no importance, who played at farming, to pass the time.

Father was speaking and the whole gallery his audience by now.

'Shanne's a good girl. I think that she was brought up in the dispensary at Merton House. She's a doctor's daughter ... a doctor's grand-daughter, living in the art of medicine up to her neck, bless her ... That was how they were bred ... the only way in the old days. It's in her blood ... the art of healing of the sick. She and I understood each other. These latter days, the rebels fixed on us, as a casualty clearing station and my wife was dead. It was a bad time in my life. She used to tinker about in the dispensary all her childhood, playing a kind of doll's

155

house, but recently we got the wounded rebels, that came in the darkness of the night. Shanne covered for me always ... called them the "sick curlews". Maybe she's the reason Merton has not been burnt. She opened her hand and let the birds fly free, as she said.

'I don't know how you failed to notice Shanne, Isobel...'

He sat down on the top of the stairs and looked very pleased with himself and proud of me, but Mick-Joe was spitting mad with him for all this loose talk. Isobel Love's mind was going at speed to pick up the dropped facts.

'Poor old Shanne!' Father laughed. 'She's besotted by the art of healing the sick ... always was.'

He smiled round at the whole audience.

'I've decided on sacrificing her on the altar of Aesculapius. Nothing less will ever suit her. Women have started to take their place in the Royal Colleges. It should come to pass with very little pulling of strings.'

Mick-Joe was mighty angry about all this talk that should have been unspoken.

'There are things better left unsaid, sir. These are difficult times.'

Isobel Love sent Bridie off to her office to bring up a silver tray with whiskey glasses ... to order rations for beer for the boys. The party returned to life.

Father did not even realise that he had burst a bomb under me. It was all I wanted in life, a chance to read medicine and quite suddenly it was mine. Matron was all sweetness and she had taken back all her ferocity. Her arm was about my shoulders.

We would clear up all the ruins of 'Polo-Pony' and have a tea served on the gallery ... sausages on sticks, gingerbread, sardines on toast, hot scones, running butter...

She murmured to me that she would come down to Merton one evening and we would get to be friends. Then she turned to the assembly and told us she had a secret too, but I already knew it from Aunt Caroline Phillips.

She had one daughter, who was a star of the stage and screen, who was known as 'the Forces' Sweetheart'. They all knew her. They roared her name.

'Maggie Love! Maggie Love! We all love Maggie Love!'

And Maggie Love was the Matron's daughter and Matron was like any proud mother. She purred her pleasure like any mother and I thought I had misjudged her. I hoped that one day I might persuade her to get Maggie Love to come and give us a show. My life seemed to have taken a turn for the better. The rain had all stopped and the sun had come out. Maybe the wet week was over.

As a background to my life, always were 'the troubled times'. Yet the growing love I had for Gareth engrossed me. I worked hard every moment of every day. The Home and the farm left me no idleness. Always I held in my heart the fact that I was going to read medicine. I would find some niche that would welcome a woman doctor and there was no particular hurry about it. My days sped past and every day produced something new.

The Easter Rising had been quelled. There had been a great making of martyrs and the curlews had been sent off to fill prisons and camps all over the British Isles, where they formed cells to work for Irish freedom still. It was to be for the future, if not now. The shop-keepers, even the professional classes, had come, some of them, to side their ideas for the green, white and gold. The slum-dwellers and the poor had always followed the Irish Dream ... Ireland and Sinn Fein, 'OURSELVES ALONE'. The shooting of the signatories started a great conflagration, that never went out.

Time was running on and the Great War began to go badly for the Allies. Parliament in Westminster began to think of conscription for Ireland, but Ireland had never had conscription. From the north and from the south, Ireland had volunteered readily, in their thousands ... had volunteered, had died. Conscription was never to be brought in, but the talk of it swayed the Irish opinion against Britain and against the Rebellion.

In Westminster there had not been an election for eight years and now, in 1918, one was held, but the electoral register was changed

158

out of recognition, women over 30 years of age had the vote and all men over 21.

Then Sinn Fein, with great organisation, rigged the Irish vote. They voted for people who were dead, or ill or away. They disguised people and voted perhaps many times. The plan was carried through and it was successful. Sinn Fein got an overwhelming victory; they had three-quarters of the Irish seats in Parliament.

So an important date happened in 1919, on 21st Jan in the Mansion House in Dublin. The Dail Eireann met and a declaration was read in Irish and in English, calling on Britain to vacate Ireland. The presence of foreign powers was 'an invasion of Ireland and an invasion of national rights'.

In 1921, a treaty was signed with Britain and the Irish Free State came into being, but allegiance was called to the British Crown and that stuck in Rebel throats and then the real Civil War began. 'Up the Rebels' was the cry and a reign of terror was on. The Irish Republican Army struck against swearing Allegiance to the Crown. The British Army was still in occupation and the police sided with Britain. There was the Irish Republican Army under cover. The land was torn in pieces. It was a many cornered fight. Brother fought brother. It was guerilla war at its worst. No home was safe. The new Irish Free State fought the Rebels. The big houses were burnt and the farm houses too. Britain brought over troops to quell the Civil War, and we had the Black and Tans, with a savage reputation of brutality...

Maybe De Valera solved it finally, but the end was not yet.

It was 1927, and Kevin O'Higgins, Minister for Home Affairs, had been shot dead on his way home from Mass. It was an act which shocked the whole country. It was a moment which perhaps brought time to a sharp stop.

De Valera was to come to the Dail to be presented with the Oath of Allegiance and to refuse to sign it. He had been given a Bible. Then the second time, he was handed the Oath of Allegiance and the Bible. He put the Bible aside and signed the Oath without it, of Allegiance to the Crown. Formality was complied with, or so they judged it. Maybe eyes were shut. They had a two-part democratic government. One might have thought it was finished, but it was no way so simple. Perhaps the dawn will come one day. I just recall the way the names of the streets were changed. I cannot even remember, if it had been already done. Sackville Street was O'Connell St and Cumberland Square was Emmett Square. The British Crown was painted green and the pillar boxes were green and the trains and the trams ... green.

I have skidded time to 1927 and left the day of the 'Polo-Pony match' in Screebogue

160

House. Gladly I will go back to that time and place. I have never understood the history I have tried to tell and maybe I have told the small bit I attempted all askew. I only know that in my eyes, Irish people had a great affection for each other, as I lived with them. Perhaps Gareth was the right person, for he told me to have nothing to do with politics and did not Mick-Joe tell me to keep my mouth shut?

So now, the evening has come back on the day that was 'the seventh day of the wet week'. Matron has gone to bed with a headache and Mick-Joe had seen to driving Father home to Merton House in the car in case it broke down again. We had finished the party and Mick-Joe was safe back to Screebogue again and it was time to end our sing-song with 'God save the King'.

Our male voice choir fair roared it out. It was a questionable thing to sing in Ireland in the last part of the war with Germany. I must make it clear again that I have left 1927 by now and back to perhaps 1917–1918, not time for the 'Soldiers' Song' as yet, nor near time.

There was a great amount of applause when we finished it and then a tremendous crash of broken glass and a cobble-stone that came in through one of the big windows and sent a shower of splintering glass across the waxed floor.

I could feel the blood draining out of my face

and Sister Sullivan's voice calmed the stampede of the men's feet.

'It would be best if everybody got quietly to the wards and to bed without any trouble.'

I was standing beside Mick-Joe and I heard him tell Sister to 'lave it to him'. It was only some of the lads larking about and he'd put an end to it ... 'I'll take Miss Shanne,' he finished. 'They may be after hurting the horses.'

Sister Sullivan was completely unperturbed. She put her arm through Captain McLean's and asked him if he would take care of me for ... and maybe take his brother along too. 'If there's to be a fight, we'd best involve the Scots, while we're at it.'

She laughed, as if she hadn't a care in the world, but I looked at her with wild eyes.

'If they've maimed the horses, I'll think it shame to be an Irish woman.'

I know there was no order about our rush for the stables, but I got there first and saw Lady Gay looking very surprised to be so disturbed. The stable had certainly been inhabited by 'Patriots'.

Sister had unwrapped the cobble from its paper and I read it at once. I read it again, arrived in the stable, and having run my hands down Lady Gay's hocks found that she was unhurt.

It was scrawled in a child's hand and it looked ugly.

THE BRITISH NATIONAL ANTHEM IS NOT

162

OURS YET, MISS SHANNE. TAKE WARNING,
FOR YOU'VE BEEN WARNED, MANY TIMES.
YOU'VE BEEN KIND TO US, BUT DON'T TURN
TO OUR ENEMY . . .

In the loosebox, it was scrawled in black
paint still wet.

THERE ARE PLENTY MORE STONES AND THE
HANDS WAITING, WILLING TO FLING THEM. IF
YOU WANT THE FOREIGN FLAG, GET OUT OF
IRELAND FAST! WE DON'T WANT TO LOSE
YOU, BUT IT'S TIME YOU WENT! DON'T DO IT,
MISS SHANNE.

It looked a wicked thing in the light of the
lantern and I was scared for the safety of
Screebogue and all of us . . . the fine house,
which could go up in one night of petrol cans.

Mick-Joe told me it was 'sky-larking' and it
meant nothing. I was to stop singing 'God save
the King' and that would put an end to it.
'Anybody can have a drink taken and do the
like of this work tonight. Put it out of your
head.'

Gareth came home that night and heard all
about what had happened. He was very upset
at such a gesture aimed at me.

'Don't think I have not heard every last
detail of the great affair that came to pass,
when the mice were left sporting, with the cat
away. It was a pity that I too was recalled to the
French Consulate. The war is not going well in
France. Now into my ears comes so many
strangenesses. You are to go to Dublin maybe

163

to read medicine. I'll be for France again but this cannot be. We will win the war and I may go home, but you will be with me. I will not let you go. See what happens, if I leave you for one day. You set the whole place by the ears. I have a house in Paris and this will be yours. You love me and this is true. I know the world says you loved Dermot. He is a dream. You cannot love Dermot now. You would have married him. This they all say, but now you will marry me. I will never let you escape me. Soon Screebogue House will be empty of troops ... all gone home, for "The war to end war" will be finished. There is a great decision coming up and whenever you look around, I will be beside you. It will take time for Ireland to be free, but it will come. Like my French Revolution, the streets will run blood here. I have thought that we will finish up the war for France and I will take you home ... to Paris.

'Just say now, that you do not love me ... and I will go and leave you with the dream of Dermot. I know there is no chance that you will ever leave me. Just look in my eyes and tell me, that I am yours and you are mine and very soon we will be wed.'

I was in his arms, weeping against his neck, whispering in his ear.

'I love you Gareth ... loved you the first day I saw you. I will love you till I die.'

164

PART FOUR

MAGGIE LOVE

The Allied War should soon be over and the boys coming home. We were hopeful for victory. Surely it would come soon? It was near enough to 1918.

The inmates of Screebogue had made a culture of Maggie Love. 'Sweetheart of the Forces'. They were never done talking about her and they kept track of her career. They had made an attempt to get Matron to encourage her to visit Screebogue on a visit and Mrs Love refused to consider such an idea. If I had had any sense, I would have followed her example. Then I got an inspiration and discussed it with Joanne Webb and she aided with me and abetted me ... said that such a plan must work. If it did not, no harm would be done. The Matron would probably never find out that it had been done. It was surprisingly easy. The officers in the ward kept us well posted as to where Maggie was and where she would be. We had only to ask them and they produced what they called 'Stage Life' ... a very professional periodical. It was easy to get her publicity address from that and we wrote to her, or rather I did and Joanne signed her name and gave much backing and advice ... even posted the letter, marked PRIVATE AND CONFIDENTIAL.

My letter was so unsophisticated that I knew it would never work. We said who we were and told her that the Screebogue patients were dying for love of her. We gave a list of their names and asked for signed photographs. It was an awful imposition and we knew how busy she was, but if she could be so gracious, it would make a tremendous difference to their lives...

'Our Matron is your Mother, Mrs Isobel Love, so you'll know about Screebogue already.'

I had finished in a PS.

'I am the CO's daughter, Shanne Gregg and Joanne is my friend. We all know from the patients, that you're due at the Gaiety Theatre in Dublin. You would be terribly welcome in the Home. I declare that the lame would walk and the blind see, if you made time to come and maybe sing to us, but don't tell Matron we wrote to you, if you don't want to come. She would kill us both for our presumption.'

Of course, there was no reply. We watched the post for two months. Then one morning, when Matron was out and this was a bit of luck, Tom Kenny arrived with a sack of mail, grumbling at all the extra work we had put on his old back. The whole house was involved as we opened the sack and Tom Kenny insisted on delivering his packets personally. It was like Christmas and nobody had been left out. Each one had an autographed studio photograph of

168

Maggie Love and a bracket so that it could stand on the bedside table. It was carnival. All discipline was gone on holiday. The men circulated from one ward to the next. There was a letter to Joanne and to me and we had to read it out ... an open letter to us all at Screebogue House. Maggie Love would give us 'a one night stand' ... that was what it was called ... if the matron would grant her the regal patronage. Personally, she herself would be overjoyed but such affairs disrupted Homes and her mother might not be too pleased. I must put my toe in the water and see if it was too icy for a swim. The atmosphere in the house was ecstatic, right enough. I never knew a person like Matron, who had the ability to snuff out a candle of excitement. She listened to the story. She picked up a photograph from the nearest bed and she looked at it a long time, murmured in a sad little voice that her daughter was as lovely as ever. 'It might have been better if I had been consulted first,' she murmured, so softly that I just heard her, but I thought she had the look of a trapped rat in her eyes and then thought no more about it. She seemed so very proud of Maggie Love.

She would see Joanne and me in her office tonight to discuss the whole affair. She swept away down the stairs and I read disapproval in the set of her shoulders...

Mick-Joe sought me out, both of us, and he was disapproving too.

169

'Are you both off your heads, that ye didn't tell me a word about it? God knows the cub may be a hundred times worse than the vixen. They're both after Merton House. That's my opinion. No man would have blind eyes for the young one. She has only to raise her hand and every peer in the realm is after her. It's a thing that happens in wars. What will you do, Miss Shanne, when the major lays his eyes on Maggie Love?'

I refused to discuss such a subject with Mick-Joe and he looked at me with scorn.

He looked at me with his eyes crinkling up the corners.

'You might be pulling your house down round your ears, Miss. Don't say I didn't say you was the one that opened the door. If it's not mother, it will be daughter now and maybe the major off to the wars. You might be away up in the Royal College and the keys of Merton might be jingling in Matron's pocket. There's black clouds that can come climbing up the skies at times like these, when all the world goes mad...'

We had an uneasy half hour in the office that evening with Matron, who said I had the unhappy knack of taking things on my own. I had made Joanne as bad as myself. How could we two girls arrange the presentation of a famous film star in a big home like Screebogue? She herself would call in the major and Mrs Caroline Phillips.

'As for the major, he may be recalled to France at any moment. He'll not have told you that, but there's a big push and the Huns have broken through. Leave is being cancelled and that's just a rumour, so don't spread it around...

'Leave this affair to the senior staff. Maggie will see to the men. She'll not want advice and never did. She goes her own way. I go mine.'

When the time came, Maggie side-stepped her mother and this caused Joanne and I great joy. There was no love lost between us. Maggie already had every soldier enrolled and ready to work at everything under the sun ... fireworks, lanterns along the drive, stage scenery, a palm court and a marquee.

My father offered to collect her from Dublin ... dinner at the Shelbourne Hotel, before the show in the Gaiety Theatre ... Gareth was to go too, and Matron. Afterwards they would have a long drive home through the night, and us all to meet them come morning ... front steps.

At least Joanne and I had no worry about what to wear. The order had gone out ... uniforms on duty. Our spotless dresses would sweep the floor. The high starched collars would scratch our necks. The dark navy cloaks would be red-lined against the chill of the morning. The white American caps would perch on our heads, gracefully as butterflies, poised in flight. The probationer nurses from

171

the Richmond might be in striped cotton and spotless white apron and the humble Sister Dora caps. These were the days when I should have been thinking about exams, but all such worries were gone. My mind was consumed with plans for 'the greatest show on earth'. God have mercy on me! I was very young. This show had consumed my brain. We had arranged for a grand piano out on stage, borrowed from the drawing-room of the Screebogue household. The stage was at the great flagged hall. The kitchens had swung into work. Convalescent soldiers were fixing the lighting arrangements. The lawn was like a circus with its monster marquee. Here people could congregate and circulate and there was a 'palm court orchestra'. There were refreshments to be carried round on silver trays. It was all very grand, and that was Caroline Phillips's contribution. It was reminiscent of the Meets in the old days and I thrust away the memory of the stirrup cups ... and the hounds all gathering at Merton House ...

Maggie Love arrived in Screebogue early in the morning and took in the array of the full nursing staff and the patients ranged behind us.

Gareth had helped Miss Love out of the car and his eyes searched to find me. He brought Maggie up to where I stood with Joanne and she shook hands with us and thanked us for thinking the whole thing out and making it possible for sending such important escorts to greet her...

Maybe her mother looked a trifle taken back, but Maggie was sending out a smile like a lighthouse beam, that included the whole range of people who covered the front steps.

She was a beautiful girl and she fully deserved the name she had won for herself. She talked freely to everybody and bubbled over with enthusiasm. She jumped like a grasshopper from one subject to the next. We must all go in to breakfast and get on with the day. Her mink coat was discarded with carelessness on the hall-seat and she trailed a fine Italian silk scarf behind her, as she went. In the refectory, she was surrounded by a circle of young officers, who insisted on her having a proper breakfast and not just black coffee. She was as quick as mercury. She was up and away with me by the hand.

'Shanne!' she said. 'Shanne Gregg! Just one whisper in your ear, for it's you I've come to see.'

She put up a hand and held my chin for a moment.

'I came here, because I got your letter. I know about you and I'll pick a moment, for 'tis mighty important. Don't seek me out. I'll come to you and find you...'

She kept a group of us about her and she lectured us in the way she wanted the show planned. She enthused about how the men had

173

'done us proud with the effects'. She had a session with a volunteer pianist, who was the envy of the whole house. They went through sheets of music and it was no effort in the world.

In the afternoon she wandered through the wards and sat on the beds and happiness moved with her and went where she went.

She met Lieut Col Phillips and Aunt Caroline and Blackie and was introduced to Blackie and she threw the ball for him along the galleries. It was such a happy day. Then she explored the whole beautiful gardens and Blackie still intrigued with the ball game. In a way, she turned the whole nursing-home into a paradise of make-belief. At some stage, Gareth sought me out and told me I was to sit with him at the 'Show'. Front row stalls, centre aisle ... we would be sitting next the CO and Mrs Love.

Maggie had booked Joanne as her dresser and Joanne was delighted.

'This is a one-night show, you know. I'm on my way to France tomorrow with the troops. God bless them! There's a push on out there. They want all the encouragement we can give them.'

The day rushed away. I had some chores to do in Merton barn. There was a cow near calving and Miss Hinchley was expecting a night call. Poor Miss Hinchley! She had taken over a full job as an unqualified Vet and was an asset to Merton Farm. I rode down to Merton

174

and we had a consultation together and I thought that one day the Vet would marry Miss Hinchley and we would be lost without her.

The lanterns were being lit along the avenue by the time I got back to Screebogue. The marquee was beginning to glow in the evening. The maids had started to arrange the silver trays with the drinks. Soon the first carriages would be arriving and the guests would be decanted at the tunnel to the marquee.

Mick-Joe collected Lady Gay and told me to run and change into my best uniform. There was a little memory of the smell of trampled grass and the silver trays and the stirrup cups and the chink of bit and bridle. I had a flashback to that day of the funeral and knew a sorrow that I could never forget.

'The major is looking for you, Miss Shanne. Don't keep him waiting.'

I went up the front steps, as fast as I could run. A quarter of an hour later, I was coming back to the hall again and my heart beat faster at the sight of Gareth waiting by the piano. He was in uniform, wearing his cap and he saluted me and guided me to our seats.

He settled me in my seat, sat down beside me and took his cap off, set it in his lap. I asked him if he had enjoyed his trip to town to fetch 'our Star'.

'The show was splendid. You'll like it tonight. The dinner in the Shelbourne was good, but the city is knocked about a bit. They've saved the Royal College for you. You'd be happy there, if I let you go.'

The hall was an enormous place and it was filling rapidly and Gareth complimented 'the company' at what we had made it for Maggie. The floats and the spotlights were professional and now the nurses were filing in to their allotted seats. This was a special occasion. The gentry of the County had not missed the chance of seeing Maggie Love. She was an international figure, though Matron had never made a great fuss of the pride she must have in her. I thought of the boys and the photographs they had, that they would take back to France with them.

The hall seemed enormous with the hand-woven Celtic carpet under the great candelabra in the very centre of it. I shivered a little at the hell of the trenches ... the dreams of home ... the bombardment, the flashing of gun-fire, the Very lights in the sky. I saw Maggie Love's photograph, tattered, torn, blotted, smeared.

Maybe Gareth caught my mood from me.

'Dublin is an appalling city now,' he murmured.

'Sackville Street is wrecked ... all bullet holes and snipers still. There's blood flowing— like blood under a door, as someone said ... and funerals pass by and faces sad and weeping. Poor "Dublin's fair city, where the girls were so pretty." There's that atmosphere

176

of lost causes about it...'

I tried to change his mood.

'Maggie Love is making her entrance from the second floor,' I said and smiled at him. 'We used to do it as children, the Phillips boys and I ... called me "the kid".'

The piano was filling in the time with the war songs and the place was packed with the audience. Maggie would be up at the top of the staircase, getting up her courage to slide off into space.

My father arrived with Matron and settled in beside us and the overture came to a stop with a clatter of applause and the roll of drums. The lights were dimming, dimming, dimming to darkness.

We had had the music of the war and here it came again now...

It's a long way to Tipperary... Keep the home fires burning ... There's a long, long trail a-winding ... Mademoiselle from Armentiers.

They had nothing to do with the Rebellion of 1916, but there were thousands of Irishmen, that knew Blighty and maybe looked both ways ... thousands and thousands, who lay in Flanders fields and would never see home again. There was a sorrow, that built up inside me. My chest was choked with unshed tears. The glasses clinked on the trays and Bridie Geraghty was in the centre aisle with her face smiling, muttering that it was the wrong time to turn the lights out, if that was what

177

they intended.

'Not yet, Bridie ... just dimming for a start ... pitch dark in a few minutes. Mind how you go.'

'It's claret cup, Miss Shanne. I've got a still lemon for you, made as you like it.'

I felt the big goblet slide into my hands and thanked her and she went along the row.

Bridie was a member of the Cumann-na-Mbann, the woman's Sein Fein. Doubtless half our people had Republican sympathies in one way or another. Had not the head-groom at Screebogue called his infant son 'Eamon' and that was Dev's name? We counted the Merton retainers as family. They had fought and died in Britain's wars. For a split second I remembered the Geraghty family, who lived at our front gates. I recalled Bridie's blood blister in the dispensary and the pallor of her face, as my father heated the needle to glowing red. She had grown to womanhood now and was the prettiest of us all.

Facing-Both-Ways. We all were, if you thought of it. No wonder it was so hard to understand it. I leaned forward and hissed along the row of seats to Bridie to wait at the end of the row.

'It will be dark now. Watch for the star in the skies.'

Truly the lights had gone down and the drums rolled and there was pitch darkness over the whole house. Then a bright spot came from

one side and a second opposite and found her
... high on the very top of the fine staircase. She
was impossibly lovely. There was a mahogany
balustrade to the staircase ... It came down
one at either side and ended up with a newel
post in the hall. The spotlights held her right on
top of the world and I thought it tragic how
people could die and things outlast them. In
years gone by, Dermot and Rory and I had
flown this same flight of dare-devilry, though it
was strictly forbidden, and so a wonderful feat
of courage.

Maggie Love was poised like an exotic
creature in a gossamer dress of foam at the
edge of a storm-tossed cliff. There was fluffy
bow at the side of her neck, like a kitten might
wear ... a parasol that twirled carelessly on one
shoulder...

The music was in the background, far away
but coming closer ... the tramp ... tramp ...
tramp of men's feet and a singing, that came
closer. Still she waited and listened and we all
listened...

It was clearer now, the singing of mens'
voices and cheerily too.

'Pack up your troubles in your old kit bag
    and smile, smile, smile.
While you've a lucifer to light your fag,
Smile boys, that's the style...
What's the use of worrying?

179

It never was worth while.
So pack up your troubles in your old kit-
    bag...
And smile, smile, smile...'

She picked up the song and the voices faded to hers and hers was a sky-lark, that soared across the vaulted ceiling. She held something concealed behind her or maybe it was passed to her from behind.

The time had come for the big spectacle. She was away like a bird swept through the air effortlessly to land on the Celtic carpet right in the centre under the grace of the chandelier and the spotlight followed her faithfully. I could not believe how skilfully the Royal Engineers had done it. She stood for a split second as still as a statue and then we saw what she had held hidden ... She brought out her hand with the old kit-bag and maybe we saw how wearisome a thing it was. She hefted the strap over her shoulder and she knew its burden well. She had no option but to carry it one more time and so she smiled and made a small grimace of resignation. Then she gave us the brilliance of that smile she had, and again it had power in it, that lifted our hearts. A sigh came from the whole great hall and applause clattered out and went on and on. The footsteps were marching away again ... to fade in distance and silence...

Now the spots were picking us out in the

front row. She came strolling out to the front seats and this was something that I had not expected. She leaned towards Gareth and he stood up and hitched the kit-bag on her shoulder to make it more comfortable. Then she borrowed his cap and set it at an angle on her own head. She had thrown the parasol away on the top of the piano with that fine carelessness she possessed. She saluted Gareth with elan and returned to the stage and the pianist was into 'Mademoiselle from Armentiers' ... and she sang it. She marched up and down and in the long years that followed I never remember Marlene Dietrich bettered her. 'See what the boys in the back room will have...' but that was a long time in the future, but a star maybe shone for ever once it reached the sky. Gareth was very amused with her act. I knew that day when he would have wanted to sink into the ground to avoid such attention, but he borrowed the CO's swagger-cane and passed it up to her and got a great roar from the lads. She conjured up a magic, that made a background for the familiar songs ... The sounds of the trenches, that were produced from a recording backstage, that could give us the weariness of the barrack square. She had brought a deal of such stuff in the props and she certainly put world war down before us for us to see and hear. She made it real for us and alive and maybe glorious. She settled for the top of the

181

grand piano at last and we had song after song and she sang with her conscripted 'Screebogue male-voice choir'. Nobody could ever say she was not one of the great ones. Her dress changed colour in the limes and it seemed that her audience would never let her go, but it was time and she came over to return his cap to Gareth and the swagger-cane to Father ... kissed them both lightly on both cheeks and was back to curtsey on the Celtic carpet, with the glistening chandelier above her head. She stood looking all about her, as the applause went on and on and the troops shouted and stamped the floor, as is the way of such gatherings. Then she wandered back to the carpet with the look of a lost little girl who has muffed her exit and is lost. She stretched out her arms to her audience and went into a deeper curtsey and the drums rolled to a darkness, that followed a dimming of the lights.

We sat in blackness and silence. You could have heard a pin drop. Then a magnesium flare blinded our eyes, but she was gone, back into some mystic place she knew of. She was gone. There was no finding her. Space had swallowed up all that grace and beauty. There were shafts of coloured streamers, flung into the darkness to entangle us and we were half drunk in the trailers made of rainbow.

After a long time, we sorted out all the confusion and filed out into the open air and the light of the coloured lanterns under the trees and along the drive. Then we were straight into the dizzle-dazzlezip-zip-zip-zip of the firework show. Over all was the ululation of excited voices and the glowing from the outside of the marquee ... and the gentle sound of a palm court orchestra, playing music to match the imitation Viennese pastries. Gareth had a grip on my arm that recalled the first day I had met him with his head in his hands near the damson tree and with an emptiness in his eyes, that I recalled clearly ... and the moonlight now shining in his silver hair. I wondered if I had lost him ... if I had found him only to lose him again. Maggie Love could steal any man she put her fancy on. I knew a sense of doom, that came on swift feet. I was tired of the show but it went on and on, till well after the setting of the moon. The carriages began to depart, one by one, and at last they were all gone. Then we had to get the patients to bed and the lights dimmed in the wards. I was asleep on my feet and I had no idea where Gareth had gone. I had finished all the night chores on wards. I fell into bed and went out like a light.

Then I wondered what Bridie was doing in my room, shaking my shoulder. She had been sent from Merton to fetch me. At last she made me understand, that I must get up and go there. Miss Hinchley wanted me at once. There was big trouble in the byre. They could not get a calf delivered and they had been at it all night. I thought how extraordinary it was that Miss Hinchley, my lady governess, had taken to be an expert in such things. She ran this part of the farm with tremendous expertise. It was not often she wanted help and she put her faith in me, who was no good whatever at such a craft. It was true we had worked some miracles in the light of the hurricane lamp in an atmosphere of Jeyes' Fluid. Mick-Joe had great faith in us and was a tower of strength, but he was nowhere to be found. By this, I had climbed into an old riding kit that I used for such adventures, and pulled on a thick black jumper. Bridie said she would come with me and we had better take the bikes. It was the quickest way to go and every second counted.

'The calf will be OK, if Mistress Hinchley puts her faith in St Jude,' Bridie muttered and I recognised him as Bridie's saint of Hopeless Cases. I grinned in the dim light from the car side lamps and muttered not to forget St Francis of Assissi ... who surely knew it all.

We rode along the avenue and down the fall of the hill and heard the lowing of the cow a long way off. There was despair that changed as we ran through the door into deep straw; there was a rush of waters and a gangling calf, that got shakily to its feet like a marionette on strings, fell and stumbled up again and a tongue that reached for it and a low soft sound of love and thanks to St Jude or maybe St Francis ... Bridie and I were deep in the straw and ecstatic. I thought it was another calf, as like 'Dermot' as all calves were at this new moment.

We all had that wonderful elation that belongs to successful midwifery, though I did not recognise it yet—a bonus of the art.

Inside the house, Selina had come downstairs and Bridie had blown the turf ashes to a bright glow, so that the kettle was knocking on the lid. Soon Selina wet the tea and left it to stew on the hob. We were all 'high' at trouble safely past. The butter ran warm down our chins and these were the moments, when such things tasted never better. We crouched in a circle round the rim of the glowing turf and the incense of the turf went winding up the sky and time dissolved into being of no importance whatever. I got home to Screebogue a long time later with Bridie still to see me safe and we were met by Mick-Joe and he was very angry with us both.

'Bridie Geraghty, have you nothing better to do, but to go stravaging mad round the Barony, delivering calves, when 'tis none of your business, nor Miss Shanne's either? There's no safety these days in the darkness of the night. We have had the place torn apart looking for Miss Shanne and nothing to find but an empty bed and no signal left, where to find ye ... just one word from staff that there was no sign of ye...'

There had been news for me and it was bad

185

news, desperate news. 'Major Chandos wanted you, Miss Shanne. He's been gone two hours now. I'd warned you myself, Miss, what might happen to him, told you that the war might stretch out a claw to fetch him back. He's been recalled and he's gone. The Lord only knows when you'll ever see him again.'

'Recalled?' I said. 'It can't be true. He was here later at the fireworks...'

'They were not the only fireworks tonight. There's a big push on the Western Front and the Allies have stretched out their hands to summon every last resource they command. God knows I've preached it to you often enough. In the Army ye're just a number to be notched on a map.

'A staff car had come for him and there was a boat train to catch and he was en route to France.

'He went searching for you, but you were gone off the face of the earth. There was trouble enough in the house without that. A few of them lost their tempers and were fighting like Kilkenny cats. I don't know what ailed them at all, at all...'

He stopped up short and became aware of Bridie standing holding her bicycle ... told her sharply to go and put the two bikes up and then go to the kitchen and help with the early shift. Then he looked at me, wanted to say more to me and refrained.

'We've got beef cattle to load soon enough,

Miss. If you will insist on doing these things, that destroy your soft heart. Anybody can do it, but you insist on doing it yourself ... crucifying yourself and me with you, like one of the thieves. Can you never understand how little I enjoy these days at the siding and the way we must betray the poor beasts, who trusted us?'

'I'm sorry, Mick-Joe. I didn't know.'

He looked at me sourly still, told me to remind Sister that I was off from eight today, for the sidings...

I found another world in the ward, full of discussion about the show. Mick-Joe had Lady Gay waiting for me, when I went down again and silence between us for a while. Then he broke more bad tidings and was sorry to do it.

'Miss Maggie Love had trouble too,' he said and then no more for a long time ... I watched the cattle being loaded and hated it, as I always did. Mick-Joe was confidential all of a sudden and walked me off along the platform to a little garden beside the line.

'Miss Love said she must see you before she went. She said it was terrible important and she couldn't go without seeing you. It was the reason she had come and then you had gone somewhere, where you was not to be found. I told her that the only chance was to come here to the sidings. I fixed it up with Mr Delaney, the station master, to let ye both have the use of the waiting room and a fire in it, for 'tis bitter.'

I asked him what was going on and for pity's sake to tell me and he shook his head and made me no answer.

Then he told me that Miss Maggie was on her way out this morning to France and for a moment, I thought that Gareth had fallen in love with her and they had run off together and Maggie had stayed behind to confess. My whole mind went blank and I walked along the platform and sat down on the seat, because my legs gave way and Mick-Joe was telling me it was nothing like that and sure Mr Gareth loved me true, for Mick-Joe always knew what I was thinking, before I had thought at all. The cattle trucks clanked off into the distance and there was silence for a while and then the roar of an Army car and the shriek of brakes and the rough scratch of gravel ... the bang of a car door. The waiting room door opened and there she was again, hugging the fur coat round her and with the silk scarf about her lovely hair.

'Good-morning, Honey!' she said. 'It was kind of you to see me. I'm terribly sorry that your major has gone back to France. If I see him there I'll give him your love and wish him good luck.'

She looked more beautiful if that were possible and she took me in her arms and hugged me tightly and I could only think of the spectacle I must present in the old kit I had worn for stable work. I had not had time to change, nor had I thought of doing it and I blamed Mick-Joe for letting me meet her, knowing I was like a rag-picker's child. She smiled at me and so did Mick-Joe and he said many kind things about the work I had to do and no choice to me, but to save Merton House. She praised me too and said she had heard of my fame and had a great admiration for me and Major Chandos was lucky to have found such a splendid girl ... and almost I burst into tears and Mick-Joe took himself off, saying that Mr Delaney would see we were not disturbed ... and there was silence in the little room and the grate sparkled with the ash wood in the fire...

I looked through the waiting room window at the white car that was parked behind the quick-set hedge. The army driver was smart in puttees and he was polishing the windscreen of the car and impatient to be gone.

'You'll never know how glad I was to get your letter, Shanne,' Maggie murmured. 'I had been on Ma's track for months, but I couldn't find where she had gone. We're not good friends and she wanted nothing to do with me ever again. When Father was dead, it was finis between us. That was the way we wanted it...'

I looked at her in astonishment and she went on.

'I recognised who you were. I knew what was going on with Screebogue from your letter. You let me get my foot in the door and she had no way of getting out of coming face to face

189

with her past...

'The OC was your father and she must be the Matron ... up to her old tricks again. You're pegged out to be the next stepdaughter.'

I was a kitten with an entangled ball of wool, as she went on with it.

'I had an almighty row with Ma earlier in the night. She knew I came to tell you and I will. A doctor he was. Dr Peter Love, my father ... a widower. Mother was dead a long time. It's the same "modus operandi", all over again. She stalked him out and she meant to get him and she did. She got him hooked on alcohol. My God! When she saw the set-up here, it was easy ... the same little motherless daughter ... She has a way with men and can't do without them. I was glad to run away and take to a career, for she's a hard bitch. She made my life at home hell, so I got out.'

'Maybe you're wrong,' I whispered. 'Father liked drink before she ever came here. After my mother died, he couldn't do without it. I had to mind him and see that he didn't neglect the practice. They were dangerous times and Mick-Joe saw after him. He's helped me with the farm ... helped with everything.'

'Shanne! It's all happening again. It can't happen again. She drove my father to suicide with what she did to him, for she didn't care. She thought she was going to get a fortune, but she didn't. I was the one who became the wealthy woman ... and she had no claim on

190

me. I'll hate her for what she made of him ... confined to a lunatic asylum for alcoholics, till he stepped out of a high window...'

She put her face in her hands for a full minute. Then she looked at me and told me she had loved her mother and knew that I had loved mine. 'Don't let Isobel Love destroy another man. She's a black spider. Don't ask me why I did nothing to help him. She kicked me out of the house ... closed the door in my face. Don't think I didn't try ... never saw him again...

'Your letter to me caught her in a trap and she's wild with you. We had words this morning and we said things neither of us will ever forget. Then she shut me out of Screebogue ... didn't want my story to break here. She will take Merton out from under you and she will make your life hell. Sometimes I think she's mad.'

I was in the embrace of mink again and her tears wet on my face and she whispered that Mick-Joe had rescued her this morning and had taken her to Mrs Phillips and that Mrs Phillips knew what had happened.

'Do your best, Shanne. I loved my father, just as you love yours. She killed my father just as if she had pushed him out of that window...'

Then she was gone in that quick way she had and I heard the roar of the car engine and the shower of gravel along the concrete road...

Mick-Joe came along presently leading the horses, gave me a lift to the saddle and we went along the hard road till we came to a grass verge of the avenue.

'I daresay you heard it all last night or this morning?' I muttered and he nodded his head.

'Is it true?' I asked him and he told me it was God's truth.

'Hasn't it been there before your eyes with the spite she has for you? We were all wanting to be blind to it.'

I suggested that we stop off at Merton and decide what was to be done, but he reminded me it was time I was on the wards.

'She wants me to stop it,' I muttered, but he shook his head at that.

'As well stand in front of a mad runaway horse. Let you do nothing and say nothing ... leave it to Almighty God. The Master is out of his senses and nothing will turn him. You're hurt bad enough the way Mr Gareth has been torn out of your arms. There's fear in your breast, that you'll never see him again. War is cruel ... always was and always will be. You've been caught up in one of the greatest wars in time ... in a bloody revolution too. It's strange the way it's fallen out and now here is Screebogue and the time's early for the ward. I have a letter from the major for you, safe in my pocket. I thought it best to keep it, till you'd seen Miss Maggie ...'

He took my horse and looked at me with

such kindness, told me to go along to the old summer house on the croquet lawn, which would be deserted now.

'Don't let the tears fall,' he said. 'The rain lasts a long time, once it starts. No matter what, God holds us all in the hollow of His hand? Rest aisy. Hasn't He plans to make you a doctor? He'll pick you up like a sparrow and blow the dust off you. He'll guide you on your way. Maybe you'll have your Parchment in five years?'

He got out the old pipe and clenched it between his teeth.

'As for me, I'm just an old sinner and past redemption, but I'm your man and I always will be. In the years that come, if the storm clouds fill the sky, just put your two fingers between your teeth and whistle, the way young Geraghty taught you to do, when you were four. I'll be somewhere about. Don't ever doubt me.'

I sat in the old summer house, watching him walk away and noticed that the trees were on the turn for Indian Princes and soon would turn to ghosts. The tears were an ache in my throat, but not for the shedding. Gareth had borrowed a message pad from the corporal who had collected him.

My darling,
There is no time left to find you and say the things I want to say. Even Mick-Joe doesn't

193

know where you have taken yourself off to, this darkest night. My signal is urgent beyond delay. I'm wanted in France and all leave has been cancelled. The Boche has put on a tremendous last effort. If we turn him back now, it will be the end of it ... and we must push him back. We will succeed and this will be the war that will end all wars. There will be no more wars. I know it ... or think I do. We all know this will be our victory and I will come home to you. It will be our greatest hour and peace for all time. I promise you, but in the meantime, I'm without option. I have to go, to catch a train at Kingstown en route for Calais ... I'll come back soon ... very soon. I'll come walking down the avenue to Merton House and if you're not there, I'll walk the world for you, wherever you may be. I will find you and we will be married and together we will put the world to rights. You are me and I am you and that's how it will be. My love, my love, my love. Love me for ever...

Gareth

xxx xxx xxx xxx xxx xxx xxx xxx xxx xxx

Back at Screebogue, the Matron was doing a good job of holding the home together, but there was a rumour creeping up the stairs and along the galleries, running from mouth to mouth in a whisper, that slid through the wards and out across the gardens. I saw Lieut Col Phillips go into the office after lunch and the secretary being dismissed. Mrs Phillips was with him and Blackie had sneaked along too and Blackie had his tail at half-mast. They were in the office for a longish time and when they left their faces were grim. Nobody had thrown the ball for Blackie and there must be some trouble, because the barometer-tail was tucked tightly between his legs. I knew there was some emergency and I thought of my discussion with Maggie Love in the station waiting room. It was clearly my duty to talk to Father. I could not stand by and do nothing. I wished Gareth had not gone away. Without him, I was so lonely that I might die of it. He would have known what I must do.

Sister Sullivan took me off duty that night and sent me early to bed. I had never known a night when I did not sleep, but this was one. It went on for a hundred nights and there were no tears. I was past weeping. In the morning the sun was shining and I thought it strange to see the world look the same as it usually did, but there was something electric about the galleries and it was rumour still. I picked up the gossip between one person and the next.

'Did I know that Matron was on leave or going on leave?'

Her secretary was typing in the office and she was a great friend of mine.

'Have you heard the news, Shanne?' she asked me, as I went through the hall. 'I expect you know all about it. Mrs Love has slung her hook ... handed in her resignation yesterday and took off first thing this morning. Sister Sullivan is Acting-Matron for an indefinite period and good luck to Sullivan. I must say I'm not sorry.'

I knew what it was to be speechless, for I could think of nothing whatever to say, and she went on with it, said she had a stack of notices and letters to type and must change the In-Out thing ...

I must get back on the ward quickly. I had come down to fetch the post for the patients. It was no time for drinking tea and gossiping, and I had no intention of gossiping anyway. I asked her if the post was in and it was and I collected it and went. I was glad to distribute the letters and it gave me an excuse to talk about something else. There were so many different rumours, but I found I had promised to write letters for a chap who was blind. He was in bandages for six weeks and time was slack. I filled in the day for him without too much trouble. We played the gramophone and talked and did all the usual entertainments that occurred to anybody ... The news leaked in the afternoon that I had heard in the office and I accepted it as news ... and congratulated Sister Sullivan with a crowd of others, all shaking her hand and wishing her well ...

I went down to Merton before supper to see to the chores and have a chat with Selina. Father was away and Dr Grogan was filling in for him. I was surprised that Father had said nothing to me, but Selina told me he was terribly excited. He was off to Dublin after a new car. I knew by the way she said it that there was an awkwardness about her for she avoided my eyes. There was a strange atmosphere in Merton and in Screebogue all that week, as if everybody was talking about me. I knew it was because Gareth had gone back to the Front and they all knew the significance of that. These orange telegrams had become part of our terrors. No family or practically none but had been at the receiving end of one of them. They were all very kind to me, even watched the post for a letter from Gareth. Mick-Joe told me that 'the post from France was cod' especially when there was a push on. 'You get a card with a few words blocked on and you'll maybe have to wait months even for that. It's not just a matter of shoving a letter into a red post-office box. It's all army issue and war office and letters are all to be censored, before they are cleared. They're too busy with fighting each other...'

It was Saturday when the letter came for me. It was with the post on the breakfast table and it was on Shelbourne Hotel notepaper. He was staying in the Shelbourne, I thought, but it might be from Father ... not from Gareth. If I had any sense I would not have opened it. I did not care at the moment what colour the new car was. If it was Gareth, who had written, it was best read in private, but I could not wait. I picked it up, tore the flap awkwardly, with my thumb ... recognised as I should have known all along, that it was Father's hand. There was a silence over the whole room and every eye was on me. I had to go on with it, although I would have given much to be able to excuse myself and go away to hide the disappointment I felt.

My darling,
This is the hardest letter I have ever had to write to you. I'm in the Shelbourne, as you see, in the writing-room and Isobel is tired of waiting for me and is gone shopping in Grafton Street. I have torn up one letter after another, looking across the Green over the heads of the Egyptian statues. Across there is the Royal College of Surgeons and, I am sure, there is a vocation waiting for you. You will find all the things you wanted since the first day you walked into my dispensary door 'on duty'. I want so much for you. My dearest wish is to put Merton into your hands and know you will carry 'the flame'. I have been so unhappy since your mother died, that I never thought to recapture love, never thought to recreate the dream. Isobel Love walked into my life and my sun switched on. Peter was a good husband and she was a lonely person too. I thought for a long time, before I replaced Louise, but she will understand. She will rest

in peace, knowing that I have rebuilt a new life for us all. I worried about you for you've known loneliness too and you've taken tremendous burdens.

I'm drunk with happiness. Isobel and I were married yesterday by special licence in St George's Church. Now we have a new family. You'll have a mother again, somebody who stands by your side and takes responsibility from your young shoulders. Soon you must move back to Merton House and soon we must let you away to Dublin and a career. Isobel will be there to take on the career of running the house. That's what she wants to do. Just put it all in her capable hands. She has resigned from Screebogue House and will come straight home with me. 'Home again.' What a wonderful thing it is. Happiness and no loneliness and your career just started and it will go up like a rocket. You'll be interested to hear that Isobel has arranged a 'digs' for you to stay, a place, that takes doctors' daughters. Soon you will be packing a trunk and ready to go.

This is good news for us all, but I feel you will think we left you out of the joy of the wedding, which maybe was empty without you. Forgive me. I would never willingly see you out of my life.

Love from us both,
Father

199

I felt the blood drain from my face and hoped I was not going to faint. I must get the blood back to my brain. I bent down and pretended to tie a shoe-lace ... kept my head near my knees. Sister Sullivan had come over to see what was wrong and I straightened up again and felt her hand on my pulse. She took the letter from me and smiled, said she thought she knew about it and perhaps it had been a surprise. She asked me if I would like her to make the announcement, for she suspected ... I nodded my head and gave her the letter to read and the whole thing was written in the kindness of her face. She took her time about reading it and she was scraping her brain to think how to put words together. She laughed as she faced the listening tables and turned it into the most interesting news we could hear. First they must all know by this that she had been elected the new Matron ... Of course, she got a great cheer for that and that set the mood to happiness, coated what had been bitter to me with a sweet coat, that maybe fooled nobody. Mrs Love had eloped with the CO, my father, so we would still have the pleasure of her company at Screebogue. I was soon expected to start off at Surgeons, so now was the time for congratulations. Perhaps they would all drink my health tonight and not forget how I would be missed in the wards, especially in the skill I had in applying hot poultices...

I got the usual groans for that and it had all

passed off well and Sister's arm about my shoulders.

I looked along the dark path of the future and thought of Gareth and Sister saw my face and told me not to fret about him.

She took me off to her office and told me that the war was almost over. The lights would be bright again.

'You wait and see. Watch the double bank down by the damson tree. That's where you met him first time. He's a romantic chap. That's where he'll come looking for you. The curlews will come down out of the hills and make a bargain with Britain. The "trouble" can't go on forever either. Maybe Ireland will learn that we're all one people and a good people too. It wasn't for nothing that St Patrick banished the snakes and put his mark on such a beautiful land ... and blessed it ... and don't be frightened if you run into a snake. They're often harmless.'

Aunt Caroline Phillips was upset when she heard about the elopement. The news went round Screebogue House, like a summer gorse fire on the side of a windy hill. She sent for me to come to the library to see her and I ran down from the wards. Sister Sullivan had told her the gist of what had happened at breakfast and she had a sad little smile for me.

'Have you had any word from your new stepmother?'

I looked cheerful and said I had a memo

through my friend, the office secretary ... dictated over the phone by Mrs Love, I mean, Gregg? It was all very businesslike ... says it's what she wants and what my father wants, except that she signed it 'Isobel Love'. Slowly sentence by sentence, we got it through.

'She's starting as she means to go on. I'm to give up the wards and go to live in Merton, as her daughter. She would be the new Mistress, of course, and this would necessitate several things. She wanted the keys of the house, doors and cupboards and presses ... labelled and numbered. Also I must hand in my accounts for the years I had the stewardship and that went back to the death of my mother ...'

I thought of the shopkeepers' bills and the notes from my customers, the paid receipts in detail, the in-comings and the out-goings, the totals at the end of the financial years ... and the taxes paid and a sigh of relief. So many times had we had to scrape the barrel ... but we won. At last we won.

'Goodness, gracious me!' exclaimed Aunt Caroline.

I had kept 'books' in the library at Screebogue and I opened them now. I had trusted my customers. My heart sank at the tumble of orders of the bills I sent out. Isobel would see my slip-shod methods and my heart was dismayed. Isobel Love, Isobel Gregg. Why could I forget not to trip over her name even in my mind? She intended to put Merton to rights. 'An efficient ship,' she had called the home and it had been efficient. I would never deny that. The secretary had been detailed to do my book-keeping for me now. In the meantime, she herself would scrutinise my methods of business and make a few straight rules.

I would no longer be on the wards and they would miss me. My full effort must be expended at Merton with the duties I had always had ... that of a doctor's daughter. It was forbidden to take the law in my own hands. I might remember the disaster of the 'Polo-Pony'...

It might have passed as a joke, but I could not see it. I had learned to take her very seriously and I did so now. Caroline Phillips was reading out the accounts she pulled off the bill spikes. She grinned at them and said it was 'a natural' for another war between somebody.

'These won't suit her, but she'll have them as they are...'

'Listen to this, Honey, you were very young.'

A sitting of turkies' eggs, new-hatched and their mother hen ... *rode island* ... and again. A Michaelmas goose for the oven ready. Marcella did it and she is to have apples from the garden for "sorce" and no charge, for it is for Mrs Geraghty and we owe her, much to be repaid, without her buying our geese...'

Aunt Caroline had never seen the BNL nor the OL nor even the OOL. These were the

Brand New Ledger and the Old Ledger and the Old Old Ledger. They had served me through the years. Caroline Phillips's face was full of tenderness for me. I had been the last of 'the three musketeers', left in the end without Mother and without Dermot and without Rory. I still remembered the order of the three ledgers, but my spelling improved.

'Listen to this Shanne ... "a good nanny kid with a nanny, easy to milk, specially for Dr Grogan's daughter. The baby can't abide to be eating cow's milk, but she's all out in a rash from head to feet."

'And this one,' went on Aunt Caroline ... 'A run of pullets just on lay, this for Screebogue House ...

'I declare they laid an egg a day for three years,' smiled Aunt Caroline, but she had a way of kindness in her. She was greatly taken by the ledgers and I thought she would never stop reading them. Then she was brought up short by my accounts at the grocer's bar trade and the pub at the cross-roads. Maybe it showed that these bills were a running sore on our financial affairs ... a dozen Robin Redbreast Whiskey, a dozen Tullamore Dew, one dozen Gilbey's best port ...

Account settled ... Miss Shanne, Mick-Joe.

'You kept it all to yourself, Childeen.'

'But look at this.' And another page pulled from a spike, and another put on it and another and another and all allowing mercy, as I had explained to Mick-Joe.

'Let her pay when she can, Breen is out of work ... and Collins and Kavenagh and Keogh and Grogan and a retinue of them, who never let me down...'

'Let her see how it was,' said Caroline Phillips.

'You had better get ready to meet them at the front gates. I'm put out with your father, Shanne, but he fired the first shot. He went to see the place Isobel picked for you, for he rang me and asked me about it. I made him go and visit it for himself, for I had already found a home from home. That place Isobel had fixed up was an orphanage for impoverished daughters. It wasn't fit for a dog. I made him pack it in and I told him what I thought of him on all counts. You'll not remember Miss Dickie and Miss Madge. They were the first nannies we had for the boys. They have a place in Leeson Street and it's like David Copperfield. It will suit you fine ... but be off about your business now. The old ladies will have a welcome for you in Dublin. It's strange to think of it ... They're part of an ancient piece of Screebogue.'

She pulled herself together and moved on to the change of times since the old days. 'I daresay your father said he knew a better "'ole," as old Bill said.'

She smiled at me then.

'It was a first lovers' tiff. Even in Merton,

205

they know there's been a falling out. I never met such a place for talking about other people's business. I blame Mick-Joe for the half of it. Mind yourself how you go. Walk proudly. Never think you have to beg for charity.'

She was very uneasy in herself and paced up and down the library and looked out on the gardens for a while. Then she took me by the shoulders and looked into my eyes, as if she would see my soul.

'I never told you. Always I've put off saying anything, for it was painful to recall it. It was the fall of the whole house. God had given us all life could offer. Then we lost it in one of the accidents of war. We had nothing, only a great empty mansion and a heritage and nobody to come after us. It was the end of the line. You were left by yourself, Shanne, and your poor Mother was dead. You were destroyed by sorrow, but you didn't bow down to it. You recruited the farm and you sank your trouble in finding work so hard that you slept from exhaustion at night. Toby and I looked about our world and we made the Convalescent Home, when the time was right. Simultaneously, we made our last will and testament ... I should have told you, but I didn't. There's nothing to tell, only that you're an heiress. We left you the whole of Screebogue House and lands, to you as it stands, knowing that you have always loved it.'

She whispered to me that Gareth would come home again to me safely. The Almighty could never strike Screebogue three times ... not Dermot and Rory and Gareth. Surely this could never be? I'll have your children here one of these days and maybe all sorrow just tears, that are shed ... and please, my dearest of daughters, don't speak any more of this today, not for a while. Just do your best in Merton. Perhaps Toby and I thought it a good thing to put a sword in your hand. You will never want for anything as long as you live. Gareth will come home and it will be peace again. There is nothing you can't do, when you put your mind to it. Now go and go quickly. I never want to talk about this again, not till we see Gareth in the avenue. Just let time slide by and remember there's a soft answer, that turns away wrath ...'

She went off to find Blackie, taking the ball from the mantelpiece and I watched her presently in the garden, saw Uncle Toby come looking for her. Then I got on my bike and cycled along to Merton gates and found them standing open and Mrs Geraghty, in a spotless apron, watching anxiously for me. She thought I would think it fitting, if she gave a eulogy about the day, when Father had brought my mother home as a bride.

'With your hair as dark as a raven's feather and the green eyes you have in your head, the poor Mistress will never be dead, God rest her soul!'

I stopped myself in time and did not say we would have to make the worst of a bad bargain and changed it to 'we must make Father very happy', and she said it was a true word...

Then I thought of what Caroline Phillips had just told me and that I had never even thanked her. It was impossible that I was an heiress. I never remembered being anything except Cinderella since Mother died. I had been mixed up with 'the County families', who had thought of me as the girl that had attended markets with dead fowl and settings of eggs, just to pay for her father's booze. I wondered if there is anybody who knows the hurts of the slights in the pride of youth. Clothes had been few and far between. I had been in mourning. Then I had taken to Mother's old riding habits and I had maybe made her ghost walk ... and here was the new car coming up the road and Mrs Geraghty in a curtsey before its elegance.

'Don't let the bitch get you under,' said Mrs Geraghty and I had to laugh, thought I would never leave off laughing.

It was a relief when the car stopped with a backfire that raised all the rooks in the rookery and I waved a welcome at the car and said not to worry.

I shoved my bike at Mrs Geraghty and told her to mind it, as if it were a horse.

'I'll be back for it,' I promised, 'but these new cars are monsters.'

I jumped on the running board and smiled at

'Matron', told her Father had a bad reputation with cars, especially new ones.

'I'll crank the handle and you advance the choke,' I advised. 'There's no harm done.'

There was no doubt that all the rooks were in the air by this and the sky was full of cawing, but the car had fired. I jumped back on the running board with the starting handle in my hand and he drove off and I hoped I would not break my neck. The kitchen staff had the front door open and they were all assembled and watching me, wondering how I would take it.

There was the business of getting out of the car and into the house and the luggage upstairs to Mother's bedroom. My throat choked at the thought of it. I remembered that Father had stuck out for 'David Copperfield' digs for me with Miss Dickie and Miss Madge in Leson Street. If Gareth was killed, there would be no question of university lodgings; but he wasn't dead, only lost, or so Uncle Toby said. There had been a great push and a trench that caved in and he was not to be found, but there was such confusion. There had been an awful slaughter and then nothing, because it was all over and there was peace at last ... I had just to push it away and wait ... not think that here I was in Merton, helping Isobel off with her coat and running my hand over its soft fur.

The tea was served faultlessly and a tray of drinks. I had not ordered the drinks, but Selina was used to Father.

The ledgers had been sent on from Screebogue. Surely they did not expect me to display my ledgers now? I had given her the bunch of keys and she had shoved them carelessly into the fur coat pocket. Now the tea table was cleared and the ledgers were to be inspected. God! Had she no mercy? Then I thought of the sword in my hand ... the wonderful gift of my independence. I looked at the pile of ledgers and knew they had been as important as life and death had been. What did I care? I could walk off any time I liked, but that was not the way to play it.

The Brand New Ledger, the Old Ledger, the Old Old Ledger.

It was kid's stuff ... Isobel examined them carefully. Father had welcomed the tray of drink, but Isobel's face was grim. He had ordered a tot of drink all around for the staff, but she did not approve.

'Just give them a shot of Tullamore Dew in a good strong cup of tea,' she smiled and he saw to it himself and was very jolly over it, as were they all. I remember the dinner to this day and Selina had done her best. She had made a special soup that took two days, and then there were stuffed roast fowls and bread sauce. There was a milk pudding with an egg in it, but there was sherry trifle too. Father always had milk pudding...

Isobel was engrossed with the ledgers. She read all about Dr Grogan and his daughter

210

who could not 'eat milk' and had to have a nanny goat with a kid at heel. She read about the '*Rode* island hens on lay'.

'Is this business or funny business?' she asked me sharply, and I told her it was how it was. Then she had moved on to the tragedy of what she called 'the booze bills'.

Isobel was obsessed with my book-keeping. 'So you kept all this to yourself?' she said. 'Had you no new clothes and no parties?'

'I was fine,' I said. 'We made it all balance.'

Father came in then having been out to thank the kitchen for a splendid welcome home. She showed him some of the bills and they laughed together, but said it was good my spelling was better.

'But did *you* ever look at the bills?' she said to him. 'Did *you* see the price that was paid for Nirvana?'

I did not see what she was talking about, but his drinking was moderate that night. He was elated without drinking and he was tired. Soon it was time for bed and we all went off. I had told Isobel that Selina always insisted on doing Father's breakfast. His bacon had to be crispy and his eggs as white as snow, done in pure lard and watched all the time. Poor Marcella would have a 'mag' if she was called on to cook Father's eggs ... and she laughed at that, put her hand against my face and said goodnight.

I wondered if I was a traitor to Mother for trying to make it all work. I could still hear his old booming laugh in the bedroom. I stood in the corner of the stairs, as the maids went up to the top floor to bed, and I heard Isobel's voice clearly.

'You've seen what strong drink can do to many a fine estate. Just behave yourself and come to bed. I don't want to have to send for Mick-Joe again.'

There was a silvery laugh and my face flamed red.

I was an eavesdropper ... eavesdropping on the maids too. I heard Selina's coarse whisper, as she took the first step of the last flight.

'I daresay she's the one he wants on board. He's been tossing on the storm for a good few years.'

Then the bold Marcella, pert as ever.

'Arrah, sure she'll box his compass for him and her own too.'

Bridie was staying the night to help with the dinner. She was maybe the only one that remembered my mother, in her own infant days, when she might have had wisdom in her simplicity.

'The Mistress was always too soft for the old Master. For all the way she had no fear on the back of a horse, there was fear in the marriage bed. A little wind was a tempest to her and she was scared of the nature of the man. There are women like that...'

Bridie had blossomed out from childhood and was a grown woman now with a great sympathy for the Republican Party. I waited in the shadow, till they had gone up the stairs and then went into my own room, as still as a dead mouse. I thought that it was obvious that Father loved my stepmother just as much, if not more than he had loved my dead mother and the thought overwhelmed me. Jealousy was a cruel emotion, sharp as a knife to wound. Father was happy. That much was certain and yet I could never see how an old man could find the splendour of love, such as I knew it. I lay in bed and tried to think it out. I inhabited an enchanted, a rose-tipped world with Gareth, or had done. I was happy, if he came where I was. Without him, it was so lonely and miserable and full of one empty, misty day after another. Joy was gone with the hope of seeing him in the gardens or the fields. He was missing from my sight and without the sight of him, I had nothing. It had all gone on too long. Surely it was impossible that they did not know where he was. I thought of the thousands of soldiers and knew one was a single poppy on a battlefield, when the final count came...

Then I started to think of Father's bedroom and Isobel in his arms. Maybe he could feel romance all over again and happiness again. Father *was* happy. That much was certain, but his love was a kind of second-hand thing to my own. The time had gone by and the war was over and there was to be no more war and Britain was full of celebrations and, apparently, they had all packed up and gone home from France. It was absolutely ridiculous how the War Office could hope to satisfy us. They had had a ferocious battle and a great section of trenchwork destroyed. There were a great many wounded and dead, but not Gareth. It was 'no man's land' all over again. No man would ever want to own it or work it with the plough. A whole generation had laid down its lives. It was not possible that ever it would come to be a field of waving corn and poppies, that grew in it. It must be accursed for ever ...

Toby Phillips had taken to haunting the War Office in London and, after a while, he had moved on to Paris. There was a house in Paris in a quiet suburb ... a house that belonged to Gareth and here the relations flocked like mother-birds for their nestlings from ravaged nests ... It was a strange thing that Dermot and Rory had been the last of a fine generation. Gareth was the last of a long line of the Chandos family, proud and haughty. If Gareth was really not to be found, there was no sire any more for the Chandos breed. It must come to an end and it was intolerable to all of them. They had started on the Walls of Limerick and had marched out of Limerick, with flutes playing and with colours flying. They had given their lives on the battlefields of France ... Vaguely I understood the terrible tragedy that had overcome Chandos et Cie. Richard

Chandos—the Sabreur...

So Toby Phillips had gone to Paris, where he had been taken in to Gareth's house and Gareth's house was a world unknown to Uncle Toby. It was a mansion, unlike anything you might find in England and servitors to do your bidding and a long Rolls Royce with a chauffeur called Pierre, at command ... and every luxury God had invented ... Uncle Toby had a way of writing letters, that had enthralled me since childhood ... the line-drawing men. His letters were alive with them, little matchstick men, who illustrated the text.

It had taken too long. We would never find him now. The years were passing and a person could never survive so long. The Chandos family had put on a tremendous effort to find Major Gareth Chandos. The whole of France had been searched. Nothing had been left undone and yet always the answer was 'missing'.

Late in May, 1921, the IRA burnt the Customs House on the Liffey and this was the centre of British Administration. They said there was a woman having a cup of tea and she asked 'the fella' if she could get her coat.

'You'll be lucky if you get your life...'

'Are ye the Tans or what?'

The filing cabinets were poured out on the floors and the lit match thrown and the troubled times went on their way ... and they got worse.

I cared no more, for I thought that too much time had passed. I had waited more than 'months' now. I had waited years, and my life was ashes.

'These Huguenots are the salt of the earth,' wrote Uncle Toby. 'Major Gareth Chandos was a terrible careless gentleman. He let a trench fall in on him once, that buried half the company. He could do it again. There was Huns on top of them. He might have been taken PoW. Do you recall him at Screebogue, as he came first? He was in a kind of fugue. At the moment, I'm after combing out displaced PoW's. It's been done before, but it can be done again. Gareth was a sensitive fellow, of very high intelligence ... not to be lost.'

I wished they would stop looking. Better give it all up than prolong the agony. Father was very happy with Isobel and she and I got on well together. I was worried in my mind about Maggie Love. It irked me, till I wrote to her one day. I had to get it off my conscience, that I might have misjudged Isobel. I was not quite sure, but she had shewn me no unkindness.

'Maggie, my dear, I have thought so much about it and the more I think of it, the more I imagine we got a wrong verdict on your mother. Recall the first history and I do not think it was accurate. I think there was a reverse side, that we did not know of. The blame might have been on *your father* and these are fighting words to say to you. If so, forgive me! I have lived here for months now and I've been poor company and they have all put up with me. I have started to think that Isobel might have been hiding it from you, the fact of your father being crazy with drink. I think she put you behind her back and shut you out of what was very unpleasant. I think she took the whole of the brunt of his death like that. Maybe I'm wrong. Please forgive me, but it sticks in my heart like a kind of Shylock's knife and will not let me do *nothing*, but leave it lie...'

I posted it with some hearty apologies and told her never to hate me, for I had been very glad of her kindness and the way she had sought me out to keep me from harm. Then I posted the letter and tried to forget all about it and the time slipped by, day after day and not one day different to any other of them.

Yes, there was one. Assassination had become a way of life. It was a political battle and an army that attacked out of the hills. Later on, when there was issue about the Oath of Allegiance, the police and the British soldiers, it was a three-cornered dog-fight and old comrades fought each other, but that was not yet, but we had the Black-and-Tans and the Auxiliaries, brought in from Britain to boost the police. Yet there was this day when Miss Hinchley and I were in Carrickboy, doing the messages. There had been trouble a few nights before, that had horrified us all. We were a simple friendly neighbourhood. Sergeant O'Dowell had been an old friend of mine since childhood days. He had a wife and four daughters, who spoilt him very much. I always stopped for the time of day at his lonely house near Killeen. If we made crab-apple jelly, I'd drop a couple of pound jars off at the sergeant's and if I picked up a stone in a horse's shoe, he was the one who was a great hand at getting it out. He had a penknife with 'the thing' in it.

They had come down from the hills on his house in the night … strangers with masked faces. They had knocked on his front door. Before his wife and daughters, they had gunned him down. His funeral was passing by and I had no option but to stand and look. Mrs O'Dowell, all in black, was walking behind the coffin and her four girls behind her, all in new black too, with faces that had wept till weeping was no more good. I went and tried to put my arms about her and she wiped her handkerchief on the end of the coffin and it was blood-soaked.

'She's weeping tears of blood,' murmured Miss Hinchley. 'How can a person weep tears of blood?'

I knew that the coffins were cheap and made quickly. I knew that people were being shot down all over the country and that barbarity walked Ireland. Even in the Royal College they had delayed my coming up to Dublin yet, said 'there was blood coming under the door in Dublin's fair city'. So now I saw Mrs O'Dowell weeping tears of blood and her life in just the same ruins as mine was. I put my arms about her and held her in my arms, but she pulled herself away from me and went on her way ... and the blood bright on her handkerchief ... and I wondered if she wanted to avoid me, or if it was my fault she had ended in trouble. My father counted as a British soldier ... and I had seen the tear-soaked handkerchief ... and I remembered the jolly Sergeant of police, who had liked crab-apple jelly with the cloves in it and it was as clear as crystal ... She would have felt no more hurt if her tears had been blood. It was a thing I shall never forget, nor will I ever forget it.

PART FIVE

THE UNWINDING CORNER

Lady Gay was old now and spent her time out at grass with the other happy pensioners, down in the pasture by the river at Screebogue. Often I fetched her tack and took her for a ride, in case she remembered the old days, that had slipped by. We ambled along the road from Screebogue gates and a motor-bike passed us and she gave a skittish sideways skip and then could not follow such behaviour up. I felt sorrow strike me like a blow and the years whirled back like revolving machinery in my heart and I recalled the day of Mother's funeral, when Mick-Joe had taken me from the graveside and talked to me about the clouds that were coming up the sky. I had no hope left now. There was no possibility of happiness. I had found it and lost it again. I must find some pattern for life. I would go up to Leeson St to Miss Dickie and Miss Madge. I would check into the Royal College and work hard. I would find all those people in trouble and in sickness. If necessary, I would take to work overseas, where doctors were in short supply. I would go to some awful climate, where life was hell and perhaps I might jettison my self-pity and my loneliness for Gareth. Was I never going to feel again the roseate world, where dreams come true, for there *was* such a world. I remembered, when he took me in his arms, my heart would beat to choke me and the moons and the planets would swoop round my head … 'Quoth the Raven … Nevermore'. I drew a long sigh and knew I should think shame of myself and did.

There was a thundering of hoofs behind me. Surely a horse had taken to its heels and run away. It was out of control … a runaway, if ever I heard one. Lady Gay was disturbed and I got a tight hold on her. Somebody was in big trouble. I faced round to see who was coming and it was Mick-Joe on Marengo, not ten yards behind me and the poor animal lathered in foam and in a curb bit, that had pulled him into a wild bronco rear, that could have sent Mick-Joe to the sky. Instead Mick-Joe was down and had come to clutch at my rein. I wondered what ailed him, for he was searching for words to say to me and could find none. His cap was in his hand and Marengo was looking at him in surprise. There had been no time to tether the animal, no time but to grip my bridle and open his mouth, but no sound came out.

'Mick-Joe! What's happened? For God's sake, don't tell me it's something else. I don't want to know. I won't listen to more sadness. Have we not had enough?'

'We had a long telegram from the Master of Screebogue. It's good news, Miss Shanne … the best news that we could get in a month of Sundays. It came from Paris. The Lieut

Colonel tried to ring Merton for you, but they couldn't work the phone down at the exchange. It came in on a cablegramme. Major Gareth is found. They have him in the house in Paris and they want you to go to him at once. Mrs Caroline is waiting for you above in Screebogue. She says that yourself and herself must set off by the packet tonight.'

The tears were streaming down his face and he not even aware of them. I thought wiser to pretend not to notice, but I was not all too sure, if I was mad or if he was. Really I should dismount and take Marengo and walk him up and down, but my head was spinning and I felt sick. There was a sound of the sea in my ears. I was safe on Lady Gay's back and Mick-Joe had my bridle still and then the green grass field flew up and struck me on the forehead and maybe it killed me. It was just the same blow, as Mother had taken. It was the last thing I remembered and a great thankfulness, that I was out of it all.

It was a long time before I woke up with cold water dripping in my face and Mick-Joe stooping over me. The two horses had their nostrils down to snuffle at my face and Lady Gay was licking my forehead. I put up my hand and there was blood, so I had killed myself, I thought. It was the same fall all over again and Mick-Joe was as white as a ghost. He wiped my forehead with another handkerchief and looked relieved, when I smiled at him. My voice was very steady, all things being considered.

'I suppose you did say that Gareth was alive?' I said. 'I didn't dream it?'

He had another fresh cold soak for my head and he had let me sit up. Presently he lifted me back on the saddle and told me we were going to Screebogue, but gently. It was true that Mr Gareth was found, but I was to keep calm about it. He did not know that the tears were still dripping down his own face and I did not make any remark, only 'Now thank we all our God' and Mick-Joe said 'Amen'.

So now I take the liberty of leaving Mick-Joe and he leading me back to Screebogue to Aunt Caroline with Marengo trailing on the rein behind him, and his thoughts on Tom Kenny and Uncle Toby's telegram. Tom Kenny had brought it in, an hour ago. There was a great amount of news and it was all good. Major Gareth Chandos had turned up at his own house in Paris and alive and well. He had been wandering in the battlefields. First of all, he had got himself blown up in the retreat by the Germans. They had put him in a PoW camp, but they did not know his classification. They called him 'the unknown soldier'. Some said he was French and some said English ... and the Hun battle was lost by now, but they had a sense of honour. He had lost all identification and worse, he had lost his memory ... his name, his number, all gone. He was obviously a prestige man, but life had stolen all his past ... The Germans were punctilious about their PoWs. He had been seen by eminent German psychiatrists. Here the line drawings in Uncle Toby's accompanying letter had gone mad. It was like Searle in another war in time, that was still to come.

I am confused about it and will never be anything else ... how Gareth walked into his own house, when he did, when he found the key to it all.

'He told the footman who opened the door, that it was a miracle.'

'There was this little red calf, that one of the cows had dropped on the Swiss mountains ... but it was sickly and became the pet of the poor kitchen. We kept it alive on the bottle ... and it was a game little creature ... refused to die and preferred to stay in front of the kitchen stove.'

I will always hear about the revelation of Gareth, till the day I die, half the cable and then the matchstick figures in a letter from Toby Phillips ... even a letter from Gareth himself.

'There I was in this hut and the Swiss mountains making a secret lonely place of it and the calf in a rough box by the fire, deep in straw and staggering about like a drunken man, but gaining strength, till it could almost pull the bottle out of my hand. It jumped out of the box one time and did a small dance of the joy of spring and being alive ... and I

*remembered Dermot of Merton. I knew him
and yet how could I? I knew no place called
Merton . . . Then I had it. It came back slowly
. . . the girl in the house near the double bank
by the damson tree . . . the girl with the raven
hair and the green eyes . . . the girl, who took
me to cook a goose and her name was Shanne
and she was sad . . . had been sad a long time. I
saw her and I knew she was the one for me . . .
and again, I knew it. I told them I had
remembered who I was. I was "Chandos" . . .
and it was time I went home. Slowly and
slowly, it came back to me and I wanted her in
my arms, but I thought "lentement,
lentement". This girl has likely forgotten all
about me. I must find her gently and pay court
to her again and I remembered that I always
thought of her as the girl who had mercy on the
little red bull, and I had desired her as I had
never desired a girl before . . .'*

Poor Gareth. He had neglected to tell me
that he had escaped from the Germans and
made his way to Switzerland and had found
a man and his wife who cared for cattle in the
mountains—cows with bells on their necks.

But as usual, I have run away with the
story. I had arrived at Screebogue and had
been taken to the library and Mick-Joe had
turned Lady Gay and Marengo out to graze
in the field by the river. I had told Aunt
Caroline that the fall from the horse was
nothing, but a 'mag' like Marcella was

228

accustomed to have. We had sorted the news and it was certain, that she and I should be on the Holyhead Packet tonight. Uncle Toby was already in Gareth's *country* house … and the family was gathering, or it seemed so.

'You've had a blow on the head, identical to what killed your poor mother. It might be wiser for you to take to your bed and let him come and find you. You're betrothed to that man and it seems he is heir to the Chandos fortune. You've been in mourning for him.'

'He'll have me as I am, as he has always seen me … dressed in my uniform, so now,' I said.

'Well! well! well!' she said. 'We'll go together and we'll catch the last train and we'll be in France tomorrow, but on the way back to Merton to collect your luggage, bring an armful of sanfoin to "the little red bull". I think he turned your luck … and we'll take Mick-Joe with us to France to keep us safe from harm.'

She took me in her arms and held me closely, told me that soon I might be bearing Gareth's children. It would set up the Chandos line again and if we could stay a bit at Screebogue, she would die happy. It was like a miracle come true and she was very happy for me, but she still mourned for her two fine sons. It was extraordinary how God had worked it out. I felt a love for her and it grew with time. Louise was dead, but Caroline was my surrogate mother. I did not know it then, but my people were to become her people and my God her God ...

Isobel, my step-mama, put an end to such thoughts, for she was the practical one. It did not matter that I had had a short letter from Maggie Love, that still lay in my pocket, lost in the wonderful news ... a letter from Maggie Love.

Duckie,

I received your letter and I went into the past in depth. You had the right interpretation and I the wrong. Poor Isobel! She was an iron woman and she kept her hurts to herself. I was sent to boarding school. I was kept at arms' length, just so I did not get involved in what a dypsomaniac can do to a house. She managed to hide up the wreckage from me. He was not saveable, but she tried and failed. At last, she had nothing to do, but put him into a hospital ... and he walked out the top window and wrote his own ending ... and she worked to keep me and set my feet on a career ... and I never told her thanks any one time in my life ... only hated her and 'mea culpa ... mea culpa ... mea culpa...'

If you see her, which you must do, tell her I always liked her. I'll come and visit with you all, when the troubled times are past. Screebogue is eternal. It will stand, though all the great houses burn to the ground. One day, you'll have a string of children. It will give me great pleasure to teach them, when they come of age, five or thereabouts, to take that staircase at Screebogue, and yourself to kiss my stepmother for her forgiveness ... far, far, far too late, though it is ...

I shoved the letter into my pocket and forgot all about it, but it claimed its part in the rest of my life as it worked out.

Just at the moment, Isobel Gregg was receiving a deputation at Merton and Father was in the dispensary, the same beloved dispensary, but very up-to-date now with Isobel doing the nursing side. She took one look at me as I came in, and had a full history out of Mick-Joe. I was stretched out on the couch and even another cold compress on my brow. There were discussions of what head injuries could do. My pulse was taken and faces very grave.

'There is no question of your travelling to France tonight ... not for three days at least,' said Father and Isobel backed him to the hilt. She sat by me on the couch and saw the disappointment in my eyes, asked me to put the arrangements in her hands. She would see transport was arranged 'for the walking wounded', for that was what I now was. I lay in bed and had my dinner up and they all came and visited me. I was put to sleep early like a child and in the morning Father proclaimed that I could travel in three days and Isobel had made all the arrangements with France. I was to go straight to the Chateau then...

We caught the Packet at Kingstown in three days, Aunt Caroline and Mick-Joe and I and it was a calm crossing. The long train journey gave me time to think of the Dublin I had left behind. I did not know that Civil War was just round that unwinding corner yet ... the most savage war of them all. The Oath of Allegiance to the Crown of Britain was to be refused by half the Dail. The rebels were to be split down the middle and old comrades were to take arms against each other. Brothers were to kill brothers and great houses were to blaze to the skies. Old families left the country never to return. There would be an Irish Free State and an Irish Army on The Curragh. The British Army would be leaving. The Black and Tan and the Auxiliary would just be a bad memory. Maybe they had been the harshest soldiers ever known but surely not? There must have been harsher soldiers in six hundred years. Some time, peace must come? The day was to come when De Valera pushed aside the Bible and took the Oath of Allegiance, but for now here was London and the sleek train to Dover and here was the coast of France and here we were sliding into the Gare du Nord and the train stopping and a car waiting for us. The chauffeur of the Rolls had Chandos' crest on

his car door and on the pocket of his jacket ...
the double-eagle, the phoenix, that belonged to
Chandos' ring on my finger.

'Mam'selle Shanne?'

He bent and kissed my hand. 'And Madame
Phillips?'

Mick-Joe and I were never ones for
grandeur, but here was grandeur. I wondered
what I had got myself into and as soon as I was
in the car I whispered to Mick-Joe if I was
going to be a fine lady at last.

'Sure yourself has always been a fine lady,'
he said. Mick-Joe also told me that the
chauffeur's name was 'Pierre' and then he
lowered his voice and said that that meant
'Pether' in Ireland. It would be more proper, if
he sat with 'Pether' in the front and the two
ladies settled themselves in the back. When we
were comfortably esconced, he opened the
back door on Aunt Caroline's side and asked
her if we would like the glass partition down.

'If we leave it open, it would be more family-
like and we can talk as we go along.'

We thought it a great idea and he pressed a
button on the back of the front seat and the
glass slid down and Mick-Joe was as pleased,
as if he had invented the thing himself. I was
touched as always, by his concern for us. He
had the same sense of belonging to us as we did
to him. In my heart, it was a simple truth, that
he would have willingly died for me on any day
from the day I was born. In this strange foreign

233

city, I resolved that if all went well, I would fix it with Gareth that I might keep Mick-Joe. I was frightened that it might go wrong. Gareth had likely fallen out of love with me and I would go back to Ireland with my tail between my legs and my heart broken, like Blackie, if one put the ball on the mantelpiece and settled down with a book after cricket. Rightly Mick-Joe belonged to Merton, but it seemed that he went where I was. I would work it out, but not now.

Pierre was speaking to us in that near-perfect English that was so easy to understand, to tell us that Monsieur Chandos was desolate that he did not drive us up to the Chateau himself. There had been doctors in attendance and of course, the French Army had had the utmost concern. There had been investigations at the highest levels and it was a long medical 'histoire' ... months to re-trace, through the PoW camp, for the Boche had swept him up in the last retreat. Then there had been a stateless people's camp, and on over the border into Switzerland. He was 'a prisoner unknown' so he seemed, and that was very 'difficile', but I would know ... how it fell out.

I gathered that the Chandos family had gathered in force at the Paris house of Monsieur, but Monsieur had wanted Miss Shanne to himself. The Chateau was beautiful and very far away. That was good.

'I think that he has had a very bad time and

234

he knew that Miss Shanne must have been very lonely too, but he himself was not allowed to drive the car yet, so I took him to the Chateau two days ago and came back here to fetch you.'

'I hope the family will not think I am rude,' I said, but he laughed at that and said they would understand. It would be all OK.

I drifted into thinking that Paris was all I had been told about it. It had an atmosphere of romance. Maybe the Scarlet Pimpernel had never really existed, but I had seen the Seine and the Madeleine, and Notre Dame cathedral and the Bois de Bologne ... and the open-air cafés on the pavements and the French 'garçons' and the attractive police, their super uniforms—all strangers, not one person I could recognise. I took Aunt Caroline's hand in mine and was lonely for her before goodbye.

'When you have rested, we return to Paris and you will meet the family officially,' Pierre said. 'Monsieur told me to tell you, they are as numerous as a flock of crows, but you are to understand they are the most charming crows, who have been trying to make himself build his nest for years.'

Looking back now, I know I must have been very green. I dug Mick-Joe in the back and remarked that Maggie Love might have made a better fist of it than I, but he was not in agreement with me. He gave me a grunt of disapproval and asked me if I had noticed the Bois de Bologne.

'There's an odd time, Miss, when you don't see the wood for the trees.'

My heart had taken to racing, when I thought of Gareth. I doubted that he could even remember what I looked like. He had forgotten all about Ireland and the time of the Rebellion. At least he would remember the uniform. I knew I was wise to wear it. French people had looked at me with respect, murmured something about 'the wounded' and stepped aside for me in the Gare du Nord. I was glad to move out into the long straight roads. Pierre had asked permission to talk to Mick-Joe and they did it so quietly that I had to strain my ears to hear them. They were all tangled up in Rebellions. When the time was put right, the geography had gone wrong. Pierre insisted that there was no difference between Britain and 'Irelande'. All Frenchmen knew this. If you were Irish, you belonged to Britain and always had done. He Pierre himself had spoken to many soldiers in the war that was done, British soldiers and Irelandais had had the same tongue as Mick-Joe. It was what they called a 'Patois' in France. It was the same in many countries. Ah, now he had it. If the Irish won their revolution, they might not belong to Britain any more and perhaps then they would not be called Britain's, but maybe Irish. It was all very 'difficile' and now he had it. Mick-Joe had mixed up revolutions with his

236

'revolution' where they had cut off the heads of the people in the Rue de la Guillotine, which he had just demonstrated ... where the ladies had knitted ... a kilo along the way ...

We drove for a very long time and stopped for lunch in the wine country. It was very sophisticated, served with the expertise of a chef by Pierre ... a cold bird, a salade, Mumm's Cordon Rouge Champagne. Pierre mixed the salad dressing himself and tossed some small pancakes, which he sent up in flames. They were crêpes suzettes, and they impressed me mightily. There was no doubt that I drank far too much champagne and did not eat enough to absorb it. I went asleep quietly, deeply, slept for hours like a gaslight turned down and out ...

I was awakened by Aunt Caroline, who told me that if I wanted to see the Chateau, I must look out through the window now. It was well into the gloaming and it would be dark soon.

There was a vista through forest, high in the mountains and far below us a lake.

'There's your future family castle, Shanne, if you still decide on becoming a "Wild Goose", but see to it that you don't run away from us altogether, unless you want to break our hearts. Never forget that Screebogue will be yours too. You and Gareth are all we have now ...'

I had missed the drive up the hills and through the forests. I turned my face into my cloak and grabbed at Aunt Caroline's hand. I was asleep again at once in the same awful dream of arriving at Merton House, with Bridie opening the gates long ago and the hens running squawking through the gate-lodge yard. It was the same battlefield of mud and mire and Bridie a child again with her feet bare, even in the cold, and her clothes ragged and too small or maybe too big. Her eyes were the best part of her, the eyes a young kid goat might have. She was glad to see me and she ran along beside the trap. They were all gone away, she told me. There was no work about. The house was a holy show and not painted and the windows not polished. There was nobody to polish the glass and nobody cared any more.

'The curtains are still pulled and the furniture stacked away.'

The avenue was full of weeds and she ran along beside the trap and there were tears about her. I was surprised that the brass knocker had run green down the front door. The dispensary door was ajar and this was wrong. It squeaked as I shoved it open. It was neglected inside. Nobody had been there for ages and I knew it was not long since I had been there, maybe a week, maybe two, I was confused. The dresser was unscrubbed. The big bottles were ranged in rows and the ointment boxes and the splints and the bandages ... neglected and forgotten. I imagined there was a smell of fire. I thought I saw a glow of fire in the sky. I ran into the sitting-room and the fern was dead and all dry dust. In the dining-room the chairs were packed one on another, but I had seen that before some time. I woke in a cold terror and knew something awful had happened. I saw the flames again, but they were not flames. In front of me the moon was in the sky and the stars were out. I could see Mick-Joe in the front seat and Pierre's peaked cap beside him. The castle was beyond them and a winding flight of stone stairs and at one side a turret and opposite another turret, but across water. There was a man who came running down the twisting stairs and it was his jacket that reflected the flame. It was only an illusion in the fall, the reflection of a red velvet smoking jacket.

Pierre had opened the car door and it seemed impossible that I had dreamed it all again. I could see the moon clearly and the star-studded sky. Yet I knew that Merton had met its end. They had burnt it at last, just as I feared they would.

'I think Miss Shanne was having a dream,' said Mick-Joe. 'There's an old nightmare she's had for years.'

I leaned back against the seat and huddled against the red of the cloak. Pierre had opened Aunt Caroline's door and she was out now and asking me if I was frightened. Pierre was seeing to the luggage and to getting Aunt Caroline into the castle and Gareth had gathered me

239

into his arms. Shamefully, my face was wet with tears. They had all gone away and left me and I poured out my woe to Gareth hardly knowing what I said, so real was the nightmare. It was the same terror, as it had always been, but this time I had an explanation for it, that was no explanation at all.

'They've burned Merton. I saw the flames eating it up, but it was the red of your coat, and it was awful and real. They came in trench coats and they were strangers ... their collars turned up and their caps pulled low over their foreheads. They brought cans of paraffin oil and the stench of it was all over the house. I had known how it would be. They knew better than to throw petrol, for it would blow them all to hell. It's the end of Merton and the stables will catch and it will all be finished for ever.'

'Wake up, my darling. For pity's sake, wake up and see this dream for what it is. It's what comes of living in the trouble of a nation straining to be born. You've seen things never fit for a child's eyes to see and a fear always in your chest, that your house would go the way of other grand houses...'

He wrapped me up and the cloak tightly round me and held me fiercely in his arms and I burrowed myself against him and recognised the strength of him and the hardness of his chest.

'Listen, little one! Merton is the same, as it always was. You have had a savage dream, but

240

this one we know as fancy. Your father and I had a conversation ten minutes ago on the phone. Merton is the same as it has always been. They wanted to see if you had arrived safely. I have to ring them back in a while, but for now, I'm going to carry you in my arms up the winding stairs and put you in front of a log fire that's waiting for you ... and pay court to you, and about time. It is past time that we went a-roving by the light of the moon.'

I put my hand on his hair and tousled it a little and remembered the silver of the moonlight, but I had no idea of allowing him to carry my weight up all those curling stairs. I was out of the car and away and I got some start on him, yet he mounted two steps at a time and nearly had me before I made the great hall. I saw the blazing log fire and the settle with cushions and I whirled to face him and smiled, but he imprisoned me with a hand on each side of me and remarked that Aunt Caroline and Mick-Joe had decided it was time he paid court to me ... and I was in his arms and his face down to mine and a kiss as light as a butterfly on my cheek and another full on my mouth and another ... and it was, as it had been. There was no change in the ecstasy that he roused in me. I found myself stretched out on the settle and a cushion under my head and I knew it was time to find Aunt Caroline and Pierre and Mick-Joe and the other

shadowy figures, that were hovering about ...
but we resisted the idea, just for a while.
There was so much talking to be done and of
course I had remembered, that it was but an
old dream.

'That dream is finished. You will never
dream it again,' he promised.

I was in a strange world, that always
appeared when the planets soared, and the
kissing started.

'If I ever wanted to carry you to the moon,
never think I couldn't do it. It's the strangest
thing that I dreamt a dream too, over and over
in the wilderness and I know it wasn't true, nor
will it be true. For the rest of our lives, we'll go
a-roving by the light of the moon ... or so I
pray.'

He went on after a while, told me it was 'the
total emptiness time', when he had no memory
of anything that had been.

'It was a poem that haunted me and nothing
else, except that I recognised it as Byron.

'So we'll go no more a-roving
So late into the night
Though the heart be still as loving
And the moon be still as bright.

For the sword outwears its sheath
And the soul outwears the breast
And the heart must pause to breathe
And love itself have rest.

Though the night was made for loving
And the day returns too soon,
Yet we'll go no more a-roving
By the light of the moon...

'It was all I had in my heart, over and over and over and I knew what it meant. It meant that I had lost something more precious to me, than anything in the universe. I said nothing...just prayed I would find it and I think I have found it and that you'll tell me I have. It was the most extraordinary thing and I saw a wish come true and of all things it happened in a wood-cutter's hut in the Swiss mountains...

'I was very unhappy,' he said. 'You know I was in a PoW camp but they thought I had some of the feeling of the medical profession about me. I helped in the hospital, but I had no memory that they could find and no tabs or identity and I did not speak...not much. I had no country that I knew of and they were in a fearful muddle with the retreat ... the surrender. They did what they could, but I did not know name, number and rank or anything else. At length they transferred me to a stateless peoples' camp and that was the lowest pit, but I knew I had to get out and after a long time, I got out, over the mountains into "la Suisse". I had an idea that I might be a political prisoner and I might be for shooting, if I were retaken, so I hid-out and starved a bit. It was a long time, and all the weeks, I cursed Byron that he had not kept a still tongue in his head. There was a great forest that I used to hide in and I lost myself in it sometimes and I could hear bells, and knew that maybe I was daft. I had a very odd diet, but I did not die. I just hoped to remember what I had lost, that was so precious to me. Then I traced out the bells, for I met the herd of cows on a mountain track. I thought I had gone mad at last, for they were milking cows with leathern collars and Swiss bells. I had seen ones like them a long time ago on a Swiss holiday, when I was a child. I daresay you've been told all this. It's been a job to keep it out of the Press. It's as true as God is true, but it's unbelievable. I was near enough to starvation. I had heard these bells far away and then one day they seemed closer and it was evening. I remembered the cow-bells that I had known a long time ago. It might have been on holiday, and I had been a dreamy child. I was an only son and the hope of the Chandos family, who spoilt me rotten. I have six sisters all older than I. They used to quarrel amongst them, who could push my pram in the Bois de Bologne. I swear to you! I daresay the war has done me a great deal of good, but I think that I might have believed in Grimm's fairy stories and then I found myself secunded to the British Army, because I had been in Sandhurst.'

He smiled sadly. 'It was Father's last effort to make me free from women ... he said it

244

himself, "from the influence of women". Then he was killed in action. Sandhurst knocked my upbringing out of me ... or the Boche did in Flanders.

'This is long drawn out, but it's a kind of apologia, as to why I accepted the herd of Swiss cows that came walking down the forest glade. I had obviously heard them come to and from milking ... with the cow-bells and the leathern collars and each with its name on and a bell, that sounded a carillon ... and I was starving and a drink of milk might save my life ... and it did and I knew myself a thief ... I had the names written clear enough ... Heidi, Anna, Trudi, Mitzi, Gertraud. I remember trying to explain to them who I was, though I didn't know and I noticed that Mitzi was taking no notice for she had a pain and it was bad. I knew at last 'what ailed her' as Mick-Joe would have said, for she was lowing and straining and finally she delivered a red calf on the forest floor, after she had lain down for a while and the calf was not alive. It did not get up and walk and Mitzi was distressed. She licked at the little creature in frenzy, but it seemed to be dead. The cows stood round me in a circle and looked at me and I recalled something in the Bible, where some prophet had blown life into an ill child. I cupped my hand over "the daughter of Mitzi" and wondered if it might be like the daughter of Jairus, and knew that I myself was dying. I blew my life into the calf's

245

muzzle through my closed fist and she breathed. I could feel her chest swell to my life in my fist, and wondered what I was playing at, but the calf breathed ... the red calf ... a small heifer calf, too weak to stand. Mitzi licked at her and nuzzled her feverishly, but it seemed a long while before she breathed by herself. "The heart must pause to breathe" I muttered, and "love itself have rest ... love itself have rest ... love itself have rest ..."

'It was a sickly calf and I would have to carry it and I thought I knew the hut where the wood-cutter lived with his pretty little wife. It was up the mountain and through the forest and it was three kilometres away. There was nothing to do but carry the calf there. I had been afraid of the Swiss. They might hand me up to the police, but that was no reason for letting a heifer calf die. I soaked a rag I had with milk from one of the other cows and I squeezed it into the calf's mouth and it sucked at the rag feebly. I was greedy enough to suck the rag myself a time or two ... and the cows walked along with me with eternal patience. I just remember falling into the hut with the calf in my arms and then no more. When I came to, the little red calf was sucking hard on a teat of a milk bottle and I was in a wooden bunk ... It was the damnest thing. "It's name is Dermot," I said. "It's a small bull calf, but Miss Shanne has just told Mick-Joe to take it off the cattle-wagon. It was the pet of Merton, for it was a weak calf, and they made a pet of it and brought it up in the kitchen by the fire. It's not to be sent to the cattle market. She said to take it off the wagon at once and Mick-Joe was mad at her, because the cattle jobbers will laugh at them. There's a good eating of veal on a calf like that".'

'"Monsieur has given his life to save one weak calf. It is a great pity. There are people who escape through La Suisse, people without a country..." said the strange man.

'I had a country. I told them. My name was Chandos and I was a soldier, but I had jumbled my wits till now. There had been a calf before in Ireland and the maids had made a pet of it. I had been Chandos and I had lost something that was dearer than my life. It was time I found it. I knew where to go now, but I thought I was ill. I would be very grateful if I might sit by the fire and rear the new calf. If they could give me the bottle and the calf teat, and a box by the fire with straw for the calf and a sack for myself to lie on the hearth. It might all be resolved ... and indeed it was.

'Oh, God!' Gareth said. 'You must be sick of hearing this. Just tell me that I haven't lost you ... not lost in the adventures of war. It was you I had lost wasn't it, and the sword has outworn its sheath ... and love itself must rest, but I won't have it ... *not* anyway, will I have it! You and I were fashioned for each other. You and I will go a-roving in the light of the moon and we'll never stop a-roving ... never, never, never. I will love you till all eternity is done ... and you will love me, but my God, Byron knew how to burn up the soul of a man, when his soul seemed lost.'

He put his face against mine and asked me if it had been very bad, this empty world and I told him that without him, there would have been no place in heaven.

'I knew what null means and what void means,' I whispered. I promised we would make it up to each other. We would go a-roving every moonlight night there was and he swept me into his arms. He swung me about him in a circle, till I was dizzy with the joy of it and then he said we had so many people to repay. Just for now we had Aunt Caroline and Mick-Joe. It was likely there was a celebration dinner tonight, that we would remember all our lives. I must meet the staff and they were no different to Selina and Marcella and Sally and Bridie. Then he himself had a great many sisters, that nobody would ever believe it, all stuck in the house in Paris at present to meet myself—and I had absconded. Was I sure I wanted to take on such a family? Personally all that he wanted was to get married to me soon. His sisters would all be fighting like cats about bridesmaids and the trousseau and all the things that mattered not a crystal bauble!

Could he persuade me to cut and run? We could take the car and leave this minute. It was a wild part of the country and the most beautiful in France. We could stop in a small simple town and get married by special licence and turn up later, 'fait accompli'.

I was shameful enough to be enthusiastic but, as usual, Mick-Joe overheard what we were planning and told us to think shame on ourselves! Just to oblige him, we did just that, and we went through a most splendid fashionable wedding, when the time came … and everybody was there, who was anybody, whatever that may mean and I fear it means very little.

That was more or less the end of the story. I sometimes feel it was maybe the beginning.

Gareth had had a long convalescence in the Swiss hut and for a time, I think he skirted death. He had to nurture one little heifer calf called 'Rouge' and Rouge had taken it in her head to die and had come back again, just one last time.

It was easy just to give up and die … but it was not easy to give up and die when a little calf on the point of death nuzzled your hand, as if in thanks. If Rouge could do this, Gareth knew he could drag himself back from the brink and save them both. Gareth had spent a great deal of time thinking of Ireland and the troubled times. If only people could cease from fighting and take to peace. It was such a lovely country and God had endowed it with everything.

Half dreaming, he thought of the River

Shannon … and Limerick, which had been a city besieged, a long time ago … the city, the Wild Geese had fled with full military honours, after the cruel defeat by Cromwell … the old story. If the Shannon could be harnessed it could provide power for the whole country and the little cottages would have lighting and heating and power at the touch of a switch … The cost would be great, but it was possible. It was there for the taking … with hard work—and peace …

Always there was the pretty little calf to his hand, sucking impatiently at his fingers and pulling the teat out of the bottle and getting stronger every day as he was himself. Always the dream haunted him, the dream of the power of a great fall of water that could light a whole land with prosperity.

The weather improved. The pass would soon be open and the world open to Gareth. He had dreamed the winter away, but it was time to go and always he wondered if his lady even remembered him … if maybe she had taken to medical school and was fulfilling her destiny. It had been a long time. He was afraid to go where he belonged, in case the door was shut to him. He had got as far as taking to skis. He looked as if he were returning from winter sports, with his rucksack and his bronzed skin and the silver hair, yet he was shabby enough and Paris was too full of traffic. The impatient taxis hooted at him to get out of their way. The town house looked like a mansion but there was no sign that it was not the same as it had always been. He went up the front steps and stopped short. He stood there with no courage to press the bell. A gendarme stopped to watch him and saw the shabbiness and the lean hungriness of him ... told him to go below to the tradesmen's entrance. He went down and pressed a humbler bell and in a moment came the familiar face of many years, asking what she could do to help him. The family was not at home.

He looked at her and smiled and she was another old retainer.

'I'm Chandos,' he said and the whole house erupted round him like another Boche shell ...

But that was the end of the beginning ... of the end. The honeymoon was an ecstasy like all honeymoons and soon we moved into a routine ... and very happy.

We spent our days for the most part between the Chateau and the Paris house ... took in the rest of the world in snatches, but always home to Screebogue. Every time we returned to Ireland, we still found ourselves travelling on an unwinding corner.

I was determined to read Medicine one day, but I put it off. We had such plans and a deal to be done before I could take five years off from the paradise that was life. One day, I promised myself, one day, but Father was perfectly happy and Isobel and he had a happy ship.

251

The vineyards in France were returning to the old prosperity, and there were the six sisters and their six husbands, who did not need direction from us. I got the idea that they watched me with the utmost concern. It was a very old family and it had run short on heirs. Gareth was the last of the whole line. It was not hard to know what I was expected to do ... and we did it.

The family greeted us in France always with the most perfect cordiality and grandeur and always that glance down to my midriff. Then back to Screebogue and the unwinding corner and maybe the troubles were abating and then they would flare again and the blood flow once more.

We were trying to start interest in a foundation for research into the tubercle bacillus, but it was slow work. We tried to start a scheme to found a hospital for patients with 'the white plague'.

Just as long as we did not interfere with politics, we were safe ... and then I started having babies. I made a career of it. The day the nurse put 'Gareth Richard' into my arms was the high spot of my life and maybe I thought I might never be able to desert the nursery for the career of medicine. Still there was plenty of time for that because I produced, or rather we did, the twin sons a year to the day after Gareth Richard—and so there were three!

I have always been convinced that I started the six sisters off on a career of knitting garments.

Mick-Joe spent most of his time looking after the children, much the same way as he had looked after me, confessed that he was starting his career all over again and he prayed God to give him strength, if they were little devils like I had been. I am always glad I had not to break the news to him that day, that there were three more sons to follow but better spaced. Maggie Love came to see us and threatened that she would take them soaring down the staircase when they came of age ... and that was at the age of five!

So in time Ireland harnessed the Shannon and the lights went up across the mountains and across the valleys and there was prosperity and a hope for the land ...

I have come to the end of my story and in it I found a great happiness—in Mick-Joe, Maggie Love, Bridie of the young goat's eyes—and all the others, who crossed the stage. I pray now that my own unwinding corner may face one way—one day.

We hope you have enjoyed this Large Print book. Other Chivers Press or Thorndike Press Large Print books are available at your library or directly from the publishers.

For more information about current and forthcoming titles, please call or write, without obligation, to:

Chivers Press Limited
Windsor Bridge Road
Bath BA2 3AX
England
Tel. (01225) 335336

OR

Thorndike Press
P.O. Box 159
Thorndike, Maine 04986
USA
Tel. (800) 223–2336

All our Large Print titles are designed for easy reading, and all our books are made to last.